STOCK MARKET SECRETS UNVEILED

PROVEN STRATEGIES
FOR
MAKING MILLIONS

STOCK MARKET SECRETS UNVEILED

PROVEN STRATEGIES FOR MAKING MILLIONS

CA, A. C. SUD

PRABHAT PRAKASHAN

Published by
PRABHAT PRAKASHAN PVT. LTD.
4/19 Asaf Ali Road,
New Delhi-110 002 (INDIA)
e-mail: prabhatbooks@gmail.com

ISBN 978-93-5562-724-7
STOCK MARKET SECRETS UNVEILED: PROVEN STRATEGIES FOR MAKING MILLIONS
by CA, A. C. Sud

Edition
First, 2025

Price
₹ 350 (Rupees Three Hundred Fifty Only)

Printed at
Sita Fine Arts, Delhi

Dedication

*To the *150 million demat holders who want to make money in the stock market and are in dire need of a simple out of the box practical approach.*

**This figure is expected to touch 300 million demat holders within the next five years.*

WHAT does this indicate to the novice investors? The shares of CDSL, Zerodha, Angel One and others top broker firms which have excellent scope and thus can be your investment targets.

Author's Note

Why did I write this book?

I lost around Rs 2 cr. during Harshad Mehta's time and Lehman Bros in 2008 on four different occasions. This was because I made a few blunders and thus could not dare to invest thereafter till 2023 January. As a challenge to myself, I decided to enter the stock market once again by avoiding the mistakes I had committed. Thus, I started investing carefully by balancing my investment in such a manner that risk is reduced to the minimum and I am ready to make it and not lose it with the only criteria being, "Invest only your own money and do not invest by borrowing."

It is not the fittest but the quickest who shall make money in the stock market (does not mean to be a quick decision maker but a good decision maker by following principles and parameters discussed in the book along with your gut feeling and research).

Research is the first and only thing you should depend upon, considering various parameters.

So, in the very first year from February 2023, by initially investing Rs 10 lakhs and thus increasing the investment to more than Rs 80 lakh during the year, I made Rs 28 lakh Plus realised profit. This is besides dividend income. Withdrawn profit for personal expenses and buying a car worth Rs 17 lakh cash-down and Rs 4,30,000 for paying income tax; my investment largely has been 60% large caps, 20% mid-caps, 20% small caps and penny stocks.

At times, I feel like shifting my large caps to small caps but I keep resisting this temptation as it can lead to a big blunder. Should the market drop for whatsoever reason as the market can crash for unknown reasons without knocking on the door. And this has happened when Iran attacked Israel. Although this is temporary, one never knows.

So, this year (1st April 2024 - 31st March 2025), with a portfolio of Rs 80 lakh plus, I intend to book a profit of Rs 30 lakh plus. At the end of September 30th, I have already booked a profit of Rs 19.4 lakh plus. I intend to book a profit of Rs 10,000 plus on an average daily during the current financial year. The way the market is expected to grow after election results, I won't be surprised if the profit touches anywhere between 45-55 lakhs.

I shall be sharing my results with you in my book to my readers on a continuous basis.

Without wasting time, let's "walk the talk" and the principles and parameters discussed in the book shall indeed show how you can make millions from the stock market.

I am sure, if you invest time in going through the book and follow with discipline, there is no reason for you not to make money rather enjoy the fruits of labour and can guarantee that losing is almost next to impossible given the time frame required in any business.

The book itself shall show the worth of my learning and sharing the same for your benefit. **Till you find the right guru or teacher, let this book be your guide as your revered and sincere teacher.**

I recall a quote by a learned successful investor that "A successful investor invests in time, rather in money."

Unless you delve into the first part of the book, you may miss the essential formula to transform your millions into billions. It's surprisingly simple! However, simplicity requires initiative. By reading this book, you're already taking the first step towards unlocking the secret to exponential wealth growth – a journey that can turn your millions into billions in just four to sever years.

❑

Acknowledgements

I shall be failing in my duty if I omit any name that should be taken as being done inadvertently.

I owe to many without whose motivation and cooperation, the final version of this would not have been possible.

The sequence may differ but all have contributed equally towards the successful implantation of this project from the beginning to the end.

I attended a class on 'how to write a book' by Mr. Suresh Mansha Ramani of Tajurbe fame and got ideas and motivation that has resulted in this fourth book of mine.

Mr. Amit Palta, executive director of BNI Noida – who once came to my office and asked me to head the newsletter for BNI Noida as a Chief Editor and that developed in me the habit of writing. That was a turning point in my life.

Mr. Akshar Yadav, who was a mentor in our marketing class and his many small tips helped my growth as a matured writer to some extent... still miles to go.

Mr. Paritosh Pathak who helped his students grow as a personality by polishing our habits and understanding the human values for personal development.

Col. Sudip Mukherjee, an NLP coach who helped in tuning our habits and understanding that all is in the mind.

My three daughters Shailly, Shweta and Shivani, their contribution in motivating me cannot be forgotten.

Dr. Neeru, who helped me translate this book in Hindi too for the sake of millions of readers who would not have gone through the book only if it had been in English.

And last but not the least, how can I forget the support I got from my life partner Kusum who took care of me with a happy smile all the way, while I was busy writing the book.

❑

Contents

Author's Note 7

Acknowledgements 11

Prologue Year 2030 15

Part-I

- Secret Decoded How to Make Millions from the Stock Market? 19
- Can You Really Make Money from the Stock Market? 23
- Why Do You Want to Enter the Stock Market? 28
- Ten Steps Not to Lose Money in the Stock Market 30
- Few Guiding Notes: Tips to Consider 32
- Risk Appetite Test 34
- 31 Basic Parameters to Consider before Decision to Invest in a Particular Share 37
- 11 Pillars of Indian Stock Market 85
- 12 Wonders of Stock Market 91
- 15 Golden Rules If You Wish to Burn Your Money in the Stock Market 94

❖ Type of Shares – Traits to Identify 97

❖ Some Tit Bits 118

❖ 8 Super Secrets Unlocked to Succeed in Any Business 128

Part-II

❖ No More a Secret for You —How to make millions from the stock market? 135

❖ Preface 137

❖ Success Journey of Few Companies 138

❖ Funbytes 142

❖ Ambient Technology 144

❖ Bharat Bakers 149

❖ Tri-city Multi-Specialty-Hospital 161

Prologue Year 2030

Avinash Nispaksh was heralded as the first Indian billionaire who started his journey in this company in 2024 at the age of 78 years.

Across the Indian newspapers, the media was abuzz with news of this extraordinary feat as he had broken a new record of reaching a billionaire status through his will power, experience and dogmatic stance which helped him achieve the impossible. A truly inspiring rags-to-riches story.

The best part was that he was still looking younger than his age and active like a young man with exceptional zeal; an inspiration for many.

The media was after him to know the secret and his only answer was this book has everything you people are asking for.

Not only that, his declaration that 95% of his wealth which accounted for just above Rs 4 billion, he donated for creating an institute for imparting education in different verticals of financial domains so that millions can be benefitted in India, and aspiring students from abroad can benefit master this promising field which has excellent scope for millions to make more than a decent living.

Avinash declared that this became possible only through this book 'Verbatim' and following the principles mentioned therein with a firm belief and with great hope that he could accomplish it. No doubt, he had to go through many ups and downs besides hurdles on the way but one thing he was sure of, as if, this book was especially written for him alone.

Once, the reader goes through this book, with the same conviction as me, I can bet that he will also, for sure - be a millionaire many times over.

This book in your hand shows you mean business and are on your way to abundance of wealth in times to come.

Pat yourself on the back and I wish the man in your mirror, best of luck!

❑

PART-I

Secret Decoded
How to Make Millions from the Stock Market?

Yes – here I shall take you to a wonderful journey assisting you to achieve millionaire to multimillionaire status for sure.

Time required: five to eight years.

Who am I to make you a multimillionaire? It is you and you alone who can do it for your own sake.

It is your own will-power, passion and reason behind your objective, which will make your journey worth and successful...

And the necessary tool being your 100% belief in yourself that you will achieve by following the under-mentioned rules:

Rules of the Game

1. Goal setting – with a fixed deadline.
2. Disciplined approach – understanding and following the parameters described in the book.
3. "Do it now" should be your motto.
4. Patience is the name of the game, persistence as well as consistency is the key.

5. Go on doing Your karma, without waiting for the results ….as Mukesh Ambani said.

6. Have unshattered faith in your vision that you can achieve your goal.

7. Confusion or doubt is the nail in your dreams; clarity is essential on all fronts.

8. Believe in the law of attraction; have *Afformation and repeat it daily (besides affirmation).

9. Be under the guidance of some guru, teacher or advisor, in any case, let this book be your lighthouse. And other books by experienced personalities, successful in making money who have already made millions or billions, such as Warren Buffet, Elon Musk, Ramdev Agarwal, Sanjeev Bhasin, Rekha Jhunjhunwala and many more.

10. When shares fall unusually, don't forget to put a stop-loss in order to save capital or use a trailing stop-loss when rising unusually.

11. Remember the rule:

    "The more I know, the more I realise I don't know. The more I understand, the more I realise I don't understand."

12. Rise and fall are natural, like tides in the sea; the only difference is that tides can normally be predicted, but in the share market, numerous permutations and combinations make exact prediction impossible—one can only guess direction through candles, charts, or patterns if at all.

---

* Afformation means living the future now – that you have achieved your set goal and feeling and are in that state as if it is real and it will become real.

13. Lastly, but most importantly, know the financial health of the company in which you plan to invest.
14. Equip yourself; It is a profession, like CA, MBA, Medical, Law, etc. Invest time in achieving your expertise, say 3-5 years, and learn the art and science of the share market through books, lectures by experts, YouTube, and common sense.
15. Be in the right company; positive environment which is criticism proof, but taking the advice if suitable and viable based on experience or knowledge.
16. Shut out negative influences, as they can erode your decision-making power and create confusion; set boundaries to protect your goals and vision.
17. Be a constant learner and reader, always seeking knowledge and improvement.

Scope & Points to Ponder

- We are dealing here with the share market – however we must not forget that in this century and in the coming decades the number of opportunities which are going to present before us in India are like the number of stars in the sky.
- Any segment that you choose, with discipline you can achieve multimillionaire status for sure.
- What we all need basically is, to do our homework sincerely. Key traits needed are: discipline, integrity, passion and unflinching and unwavering faith in our vision.

- Guiding philosophy—How can I create opportunities for my friends, colleagues or customers alike? Or for any person who approaches for guidance. How could my expertise be of assistance? At least not to harm anyone's interest. Our attitude and action should be based on giver's gain philosophy.
- When we work with givers gain philosophy – opportunities shall crop up automatically without our seeking the same. What goes around comes around.

❑

Can You Really Make Money from the Stock Market?

Definitely, the answer is Yes.

It is true. Absolutely true. When you wish to start any business, you need to invest in capital. Right? So here I have, at the age of 78 years, learnt that instead of starting your own business, go on buying shares of two or three companies whose business you understand. Whose business has future scope, which has government backing, which is already there in the trade for quite some time and doing fantastic and has future growth. This book includes a number of parameters which a company must go through before one can think of investing in such a company, in order to make money or not to lose money. When the pass percentage is more than 90%, one can just start investing - stepwise on every fall or rise in SIP mode.

No doubt, at times one must use one's power of judging the future of new technology and putting one's life into it because one has immense confidence in innovation and new technology. There is a possibility that you won't find any precedent available. Rather it is an opportunity to create one precedent. Case in point is that of Rakesh Jhunjhunwala who started buying shares of Titan and made Rs 11,000 crores in this share alone by investing Rs 18 crores.

However, before starting investing, one must be clear as to why he is entering the stock market? It is to make 20% + returns over a particular period or such other goals? That must be put down in writing with a dead line fixed. For without fixing a dead line the goal has no meaning whatsoever. In the same way, the quantity of money to be earned, should also be fixed for any vivid or hazy goal cannot be a goal. Another thing which we must remember is **never change the goal – change the strategy**.

So, it is essential to keep in mind this aspect, for the simple reason you don't need to love the share but money through that share. So, one has to develop the strategy and to my mind the strategy has to be such that we go on making money side by side when the shares are on the high and buy when the share is down. Question arises how much to sell and how much to buy? So, my line of action has been, say, in the case of Suzlon where I am very optimistic, I have been increasing my stake from time to time and selling the shares above 10,000 shares quantity over a period of time thus adding to profit. Thinking that 10,000 shares are for long term and rest I have so far gone up to 39,000 shares and latest sold 4000 once and 5000 once and have booked profit say at 43.70 and when the price is again 42 and shall be adding another 5000 or so from time to time, if at all when it goes down below 41 or near about.

This way so far, I have booked more than Rs 3 lakh profit during the last one year and today the amount invested is around Rs 12 Lakh plus. (As on today, 2nd August, the share price of Suzlon has come around Rs. 71)

In the same way, I had started investing in IRFC and have already made a profit of Rs 5 lakh plus realized and have a corpus of around 2000 shares which I have kept for long term. Shall add when the price shall fall and sell the same when the price may go up. This way I have been adding to my kitty of profit realized with a target Rs 10,000 per day minimum in any case on an average.

Last year had made a profit of Rs 28 lakh plus and paid Rs 430000 advance tax being on short term profit booked.

This year has a target to make a profit of Rs 45 lakh plus on average investment of Rs 80-90 lakh portfolio.

It all needs churning the shares and booking profit from time to time.

I know that in the share market one needs to invest for the long-term to make good profit, in crores or 100 times your investment.

Another lesson I have learned during this period is, keeping into consideration my age being 78 years plus, I have to go on booking profit and cannot think of long term; as it is futile and for whom? So, working on the principle that at least 30% shares should be for long term and rest for buying and selling in order to book profit as mentioned above.

One learns every day and for the same purpose have decided to pen down my experience in my own simple way to make young enthusiastic one's to start investing with a clear purpose that if they follow the advice, they cannot lose money **provided**, they strictly follow the parameters discussed and one of them being the most important 'never borrow' for investing in shares, come what may. Secondly, never invest without thoroughly understanding the company and business you're investing in. Always conduct reasonable research on the company and have a clear rationale for your investment decision.

I shall share one of the incidents way-back in 2008 when I had Rs 80 lakh and I had studied a lot about shares and selected to buy shares of ten companies which were to give bonus. Under the greed, I borrowed Rs 35 lakh from INDIA BULLS with the intention to clear off by selling the original shares partly and clearing off the loan.

However, with total shares being Rs 1,15,00,000 which included Rs 35 lakh loan, Lehman Brothers of USA happened and the index came down from 21000 or so to 9000 within a week with the result that my shares of 1.15 cr. came down to Rs 55 lakh which included a loan of Rs 35 lakh and thus wiping off my 60 lakhs of capital within a week. To save the balance 20 lakhs, I lost another Rs 10 lakh, net result being lost Rs 70 lakh within a week and thus I vowed never to enter the stock market.

This sort of situation can arise knocking on our door without prior notice. So never be overconfident.

Ironically, it is often the expert swimmer or best swimmer who is most likely to be drawn to reckless behavior, not due to lack of skill, but to show off or prove their exceptional bravery.

Making money in the share market can seem like a mirage for impatient, greedy, or reckless investors. However, history shows that top companies consistently offer opportunities to buy low and sell high. To succeed, learn when to buy and sell through experience, and:

1. Choose companies with strong parameters (as outlined in this book).
2. Be patient and wait.

With a disciplined approach, the share market rewards long-term investors."

For the simple reason, when the USA market falls or rises does the company's parameters change? Over a long-term period? Generally, not. Yes, at times it can have an effect and this must be considered on the merits it may have. For instance, if a large bank fails and is a client of our big IT company and that too a major one, it will definitely cause an impact and thus we need to change our investment strategy. Similarly, there can be so many ifs and buts and what we need is to slightly adjust our strategy accordingly in a short run without fear.

Similarly, when out of the top five stocks which form more than 5% of the index in large cap go down, it affects the whole share market, does it change the parameters of mid-cap shares? No and still they also fall in line... So, one can understand that this is mostly temporary and with time it shall come to its original state.

"The market owes you nothing. Take full responsibility for everything that happens and your results will improve."

– Dan Zanger

❑

Why Do You Want to Enter the Stock Market?

Money is not God but not less than God too. On every step of the way we need money. There is no respect if we do not have money.

So, I have earned millions and lost millions too, not only in business but in the share market too.

To my mind it is difficult to make money or earn money, till you make it... once you make it, you feel how easy it was, and all those who are not making are fools. Our perception changes so often, that it is difficult to believe this aspect of human behaviour.

Having lost enough money through my own mistakes on various occasions during my prime life and know that you generally have a circle according to the standard you develop. Here I remember a quote – "Your company matters; when you are in the company of five scoundrels you are the sixth one. And in case you are in the company of five millionaires you are the sixth one."

So as a challenge to myself at this age of 78, I decided to make money through this mode, as I know this is the only way where with proper guidance and patience one can not only make a nice living but get fabulously rich in due course of time, keeping in view compounding principle of Albert Einstein. Today I have realized that to make millions this principle can be handy, provided the same is used with extreme care vision, focus on understanding the company to which the relevant share or stock belongs.

Breed matters.

At the outset let me make it clear, I don't have the urge to make millions but I am taking it as a challenge to myself that even now I can do it. And that is precisely my main aim to see and share my knowledge for all those who have entered the share market or are going to enter and as usual are going to commit the same mistakes I did.

"Know what you own, and know why you own it."

– Peter Lynch

❑

Ten Steps Not to Lose Money in the Stock Market

1. See your investment is in large cap shares only.
2. See that the share identified by you / recommended by experts passes the TEST of PARAMETERS by at least 80%–90% marks.
3. That you have spread your investment in at least five shares in different segments.
4. That you have kept 20% of your investment in hard cash – to invest when shares go down.
5. That you invest in parts while the going is upward or downward (in both cases)
6. That you have not borrowed funds to invest.
7. That you don't love your investment emotionally – you go on booking profit side by side (depends upon your risk appetite also which is dealt-in with separately).
8. Out of total investment, you should keep half of the investment for long term and half for buying and selling (shall be dealing in detail in another chapter)
9. Have your goal defined as to earning in a particular stock say 25% and go on selling at least half when reach that goal—and buy on dip if it presents opportunity again

10. You have given fair marks to your investment while giving scores without bias.

It does not mean that we should never invest in mid-caps or small caps or penny stocks.

It simply makes us aware as to our risk appetite and the object of how much money we want to make. There is a test devised as to risk appetite and that can be undertaken which has been put in as annexure A

"People who invest make money for themselves; people who speculate make money for their brokers."

– Benjamin Graham

❑

Few Guiding Notes: Tips to Consider

- Invest only when you are ready to lose money.
- Invest only if you have tons of patience.
- Have the parameters checked; 31 in total, not necessary in a proper sequence.
- Fall in the market or in a particular share is an opportunity …. So, cherish it.
- Trend should be known – Go with the trend – enjoy and capitalise the same. If it is upward, it won't last forever…and vice versa.
- Government policy is as important as the parameters.
- Actually, there is no secret – but common sense which is usually uncommon.
- Form is temporary- class is permanent.
- Love money- not the stock.
- Long term vs short term – one's horizon has to be short-term or long-term depending upon one's mission and age-goal and satisfaction quotient.
- Age matters.
- Wisdom is a mirage – learning never stops… It will help.

- You will always get a chance – so just chill – generally when share goes up – you feel you have missed the opportunity – it is not so- you will get the chance provided you are ready to grab the same …when downward trend follows….
- One can never know the bottom …. So, start buying now … and go on adding on every fall or on every rise.
- Experience matters but facts, news and data is as important as air to live
- Don't act on rumours or on emotions – check the facts first before initiating action
- Try to categorise the shares according to its gene. Its traits which one can understand after going through the chapter on type of shares
- Interpretation of a particular situation matters – depends upon one's experience – history of that share-government policy- seasonal demand – international presence – change in management- ethics- integrity of the management and so on. One can see the glass half empty or one can see the glass half full.
- Most of us see things differently and none of us are to be blamed. That is a hard fact of life.
- All of us have the same tongue, but our tastes differ. So, we must agree to differ.

"Human is always subject to his own emotion. How many of us can break free from the greed, fear, and unfounded hope that are so common in the stock market?"

– Benjamin Lee

❑

Risk Appetite Test

Annexure "A"

To measure one's risk appetite quotient

Take the following test before you enter the arena - in a world of making money.

1. Why do you want to enter the stock market?

    A. To make reasonable money

    B. To get quick rich

    C. To lose money

    D. To experiment and gain knowledge

    E. To achieve billionaire status within a decade plus time

2. What is your risk appetite?

    A. If stock falls 25%, what will you do?

    B. If stock rises 30% in three months, what will you do? Buy more or sell?

    C. If there is all across selling, what will you do?

    D. If you get a good tip from a friend – how much will you buy in % of your investment portfolio? If at all.

    E. Or you will pass the tip or enquire from people dealing in shares- friends or seniors

F. Or on receiving the tip, you will start researching the company and analyse the same as per parameters of a quality stock. And then take a call based on your own study.

G. Which of the following you will follow?

	Large Cap	Mid Cap	Small Cap
1.	50%	25%	25%
2.	60%	20%	20%
3.	75%	15%	10%
4.	100%	00	00
5.	33%	33%	33%

Where in large cap the risk is 10%, in mid cap the risk of losing is 40% and in small stocks or penny stocks the risk of losing is anywhere from 60% to 100%.

However, given a time frame of a couple of years if the parameters of some penny stocks are of grade A and can pass through most of the tests or parameters described in next chapter can give multi-time returns. So, the main issue is, how to select the same?

My approach has been in such cases for trials I buy as if I am spending on lunch either in Dhaba or five-star, depending upon type of share and forget the investment.

As my knowledge and experience about the share increases, I start adding or getting out completely. For the simple reason there is no dearth of good shares which can give you better returns.

I did select Salasar technology – synformulation-integra essential – Infibeam Avenue – Radhika Jewellers – Vikas life care and Vikas Echo – it is a thrill at times. So, one can decide the same as per his or her risk appetite or bent of mind as to how one thinks and not taking to heart any unusual loss if at all it occurs.

Decisions can be wrong as I recall when President Roosevelt once said, “75% of the time I thought I was right- I was wrong” so where do we stand? Out of the above five shares in the first three I have made good profits too. And last two Vikas life and Vikas echo are still laying down in slumber.

Invest in risk free stocks? Are there any? There cannot be, however one can reduce the risk by selecting the best ones which pass through most of the tests from all angles. This comes from knowledge and experience, thus can serve the purpose to a large extent by reducing the risk to the minimum, that is all.

> *“If you wait for the right time to buy, you’ll never buy anything at all. And if you sell when everyone says sell, you’ll never have anything at all.”*
>
> **– Jan Somers**

❑

31 Basic Parameters to Consider before Decision to Invest in a Particular Share

1. Management Stake

The company which we are dealing with now, we have to see what is the stake of the management? Is it more than 50%? In normal circumstances this should be the very minimum and it being so we need to give it say one point and if it is 55%, 2 points and for every 5% additional another one point so if the company has 75% share with the management it should be 5 points.

In cases where the management is increasing its stake from time to time, it should mean positive development. The more the stake by the management on the increasing side, more is the positive effect on the investment criteria being on the positive side.

There are exceptional cases such as Suzlon, Reliance Power. Rattan India Power and many more where companies have started giving good results but stake of management is scanty or pledged. These classes of companies need special study.

In case the management has increased its stake after having 50% plus and additionally 2 points must be given for every increase of 5% stake.

In case management has pledged its shares – one point must be deducted for every 5% stake

In case management has sold its shares for personal use 2 points for every sale of 5% must be deducted and if it is reduced from the 50% downwards straight away don't consider investing in the said company provided the shares have been picked by the financial institutions.

Needless to say, there may be exceptions – and that depends upon if the stake sale is to some MNC or TATA or Reliance or some big business group of repute the whole scenario changes and one may have additional incentive to increase its stake in the said company and our whole exercise becomes easy rather an opportunity not to be missed.

However, here we assume that the information has substance and is confirmed by the company taking over and not a trap!

Here we need to discuss the sale of stake by the government when it is going to dilute its stake to bring it down to 75% as per law. Case of IRFC and other government companies can be a good example.

In such cases, one has to see other parameters and under that lens the decision can be made… some cases can be studied to get clarity.

It is most important that a good management stake in the company is an ideal indication as to the strength of the company. It shows that management has a positive attitude and hope for doing better in the coming years.

However, future outcomes depend on multiple factors, including product demand, its applications across various industries, and the company's market share both domestically and internationally. Only actual results will reveal what will happen.

If the management of the company is increasing its stake it is even better, and if it is reducing its stake (except for the reason to reduce to comply with regulatory reasons) it can point out danger signals. Except when in order to expand its capacity and in order to avail loan by pledging its shares for meeting margin money criteria. Though caution is the watchword when shares are being pledged.

Or for some emergency which cannot be revealed for one reason or the other – such as division among partners and taking over of the company by one or more directors.

There can be various other reasons and to know them can be helpful in deciding the investment strategy.

2. Profit and Growth

The value of the company shows its worth only by performance not by its name or management capability. Performance speaks and results in price movement in the market. Better the performance more the reward.

So, the best way is to see the pattern of the company's profit and growth for the last three years at-least.

If the company is growing in sales by 15% or more for the last three years – reward it with a + sign.

Similarly, it is showing growth in profits above 15% consistently for the last three years. The same formula should be applied here too as above.

Basic point is whatever is the growth pattern depending upon industry to industry it is growing upward consistently on both counts profit wise and growth wise.

There can be exceptions to this rule depending upon the industry to industry and that point has to be considered. For if the company is running in losses and has large debt- but now it has started making profit and its liability is being reduced one way or the other – that shall make a lot of difference and shall change the whole game of awarding points.

These things have to be considered on broader parameters on case-to-case basis.

In the case of an NBFC company the liability has a significance in a different manner. More the loan, more may be profits and thus need to calculate the liability of the company under a different light. Under a different perspective or lens.

3. Volume of Shares

Consider the following factors:

1. Trading frequency: daily, weekly, or monthly
2. Percentage of shares delivered
3. Listing status: Indian exchanges, NASDAQ, or other international markets
4. Trading restrictions: circuit breakers, Additional Surveillance Measure (ASM) list, or under surveillance

All these factors significantly impact investment decisions.

The same shall help in deciding the liquidity of the stock and as to dependability as to any time one can liquidate one's share from its portfolio.

Before that, it may help us to know as to the number of shares the said company has overall. And the number of shareholders.

If there is consistent volume of trading it means more people are aware of the company's existence and thus can add to its popularity which can thus be a point in favor of the company.

More volume trading also means more liquidity of the share.

If the volume starts increasing in trading, it means something is about to erupt; there may be a surprise or two, such as some big contract, bonus shares or good dividend. May be many other reasons such as taking over of the company by the said company or being taken over by some MNC or local big daddy.

All these indications in advance may be a set-up to fleece the innocent investors – depending upon some sharks who can manipulate the market in case of small companies or even big companies. We need to be extra careful – for that is the name of the game in the share market.

9 out of 10 people lose money in the share market while opening ICICI.DIRECT.COM warns.

So, it is their experience which speaks. We should give due regard.

Money in the share market evaporates faster than one can think.

You intend to make it big, and here it is, you see your share portfolio being reduced to dust in no time, for one small mistake and everything turns up-side-down.

Timing of your investment matters. Never put your eggs in one basket.

I recall last month (April 2024) I bought shares of TATA investment and suddenly when they reached from Rs 1800 to Rs. 5000 I thought of booking some profit- but due to laziness skipped the action, and here it was daily upper circuit till it reached 9700 per share.

Then suddenly news dropped like a bomb that there is no IPO by Tata Sons and share price started a roller coaster ride downward with lower circuit. Till it reached just in the range of Rs 6,000 - Rs 7,000. And this hide and seek went on for some time and now it is on - in consolidation mode.

Share market is a mirage... or a place where with some common sense and patience, one can make not only millions but billions.

Only timing should be known – like predicting when the earthquake shall occur? Such predictions and uncertainty are rewarded or punished.

With experience one may at times predict even the coming earthquake… animals and birds do know it before it comes. That smelling sense generally develops who have bettered through gaining and losing during their lifetime and still surviving and in a much better way.

There is no quick money – either in share market or otherwise- only thing is your belief in yourself and logical steps with conviction you undertake despite the whole world against you.

Case in point is Mukesh's decision to launch JIO with conviction and confidence keeping in mind the demand and perception of the data market in India.

Your vision today in 2024 as to what will happen to shares of Railways- NBFC companies such as Jio Finance, IRFC, Suzlon, Rites, chemical companies which are lying dormant because of cyclical nature like a sleeping Giants. Shares of defence or shipping companies, freight and in manufacturing line say in 2030 and lo, you can hit a jackpot.

Power shares- AI technology shares like Affle, Tata Elxsi, Tata Technology and many more, the list is endless and scope unlimited.

Your decision to hold on, few of these shares according to your wits and judgment can help you make millions in proportion to your investment and holding time.

4. Investment by Domestic as well as International Financial Institutions besides by Government of India and Mutual Funds.

This is another indication as to a growing company with a promise to deliver in terms of dividends, and return to the investors.

To know how many domestic institutional investors are buying a particular stock can be interpreted favorably by the retail investors. Keeping into consideration related other factors.

Any single reason out of 31 parameters or more can be hazardous, as one never knows the mind of the operators who are way far ahead without doubt, as compared to novice or normal investors, who know the psychology of retail investors better than most of us.

Simple example: when a shopkeeper says 30% discount for today only- our intention or mind goes in for we don't want to miss the opportunity- whereas his daily modus operandi is the same. Someone or the other is hooked and thus his business starts roaring. But not for long enough.

News filtration technique must be learnt in order to avoid and give you advance signal as to how much % of share capital they are investing in a particular company? In order to decide as to how much stake one should put in out of his total corpus? Generally, one should not invest more than 10% of one's capital in any single company unless and until it is a business decision and participating or non-participating one.

Similarly, the more the investment by the financial institution, the better it is and one can in normal circumstances take it as a green signal to go ahead for investing in this particular company.

However, one needs to keep watch as to when financial institutions decide to reduce their stake in that particular company and reason thereof, if you can trace, for the reason may be to book profit or they may see a red signal as they would have generally a nominee director on the board of the said company and would know the danger if any, in advance.

Every decision has to be taken after due deliberation as to other factors – monopoly status of the company being in danger, a competent adversary entering the industry which shall reduce company's market share and as such impact thereof on the profits and so on.

Government raiding for reasons of money laundering, tax concealment or for any other reason have to be taken into account either temporarily or on a permanent basis.

Increasing or decreasing stake by the financial institutions has to be given weight it deserves.

5. Strategy Formulation

In this we shall be discussing our strategy to deal with different situations and circumstances and why?

How to decide under various situations and logic behind the same?

a) When others follow a particular share, our mind should be on a different one which is dormant but how to identify the same? Or we can call it identifying a sleeping beauty.

b) Our why? Need to be clear as to why we are investing? How much are we investing and what return are we expecting? Is it for the short term? Or is it for the long term?

c) Depending upon our target- we need to decide as to how much quantity we need to keep up for long-term and how much to keep for short-term.

d) Churning off stock is an art. Profit is the one which has come to our pocket or in our bank account. Not the notional gain …

e) Regularly booking profits by selling a specific amount of shares daily or weekly can be a prudent approach. This strategy helps avoid regret over not selling and can provide consistent returns. If the stock continues to rise after you've sold, it shouldn't be a major concern for two reasons:

    1. You couldn't have known with certainty that it would rise further.

    2. It's impossible to accurately predict a stock's peak price.

f) Remember, all stocks eventually experience a downturn, which can present new opportunities to profit. This cyclical nature of the market underscores the value of a disciplined profit-booking strategy.

g) Your money realised from the sale of share, including profit you must have invested in some other stock after due consideration and that rise there has to be some figure, thus compensating for the notional profit you would have seen in the price against share sold, not in your pocket.

So, the satisfaction level develops in such a manner that every week profit booked is your prize and is in your bank or in some share.

h) How much return are we targeting? And in how much time? And thus, we need to go on booking the profit partially in any case.

We need to remember that most shares shall see the pattern of rise and fall and with time we shall through our experience or gut feeling as the time passes shall be aware of such tides and can thus decide to offload partially and add on every fall so that without affecting the portfolio we add to our income to enjoy and cherish side by side.

The other approach can be set out with certain shares as a long term for the time being and go on adding from the profit from other shares – such as from large caps – mid caps and small caps. Thus, building up the portfolio on strong footings.

Bear Market?

"A 6 to18 month period when the kids get no allowance, the wife gets no jewelry and the husband gets no sex."

– **Anon**

i) How to insulate the portfolio from pirates or big operators who will lay the trap in most cases to investors disadvantage from time to time. Need to develop some system to get early warning and thus be in a cautious mode to halt such victimisation unnecessarily.

Examples of shares – history and how much it has given to the investors? During 10 years of time and less ….

Therefore, one thing is certain and that is:

Given time, patience and persistence, your investment is going to reward you provided you have taken cognizance of the parameters discussed in this book.

Generally, most of TATA-Group shares are going to reward you handsomely in due course of time, as they enter the business after due research on all aspects of business, demand, world's present scenario and future of the industry vis-a-vis demand and supply of the product in various sectors, various regions, locally as well as internationally.

They also know what R & D is going on in a particular industry and at any time fate can change and fear of obsoleteness of current machinery is going to be the ultimate outcome. So necessary steps to insulate such expected changes will be taken care of to reduce the losses if any due to such abrupt changes.

I remember in 1967, if I am not wrong, Government had decided to devalue rupee considerably in order to increase exports- TATA was the only company which had insurance against devaluation and thus its import bill of machinery was not affected whereas those others had to pay high price against imports which disturbed their profitability to large extent.

6. Forget shares and put them under a separate category

This means where we have made good profits and balance shares, we have in our portfolio are free to us. It is advised to Put them under a separate group in a second demat account where you have only shares, which are free to you (after evaluating them one by one on different parameters and giving them star category say 5 Star – 4 Star etc. for very safe ones like Tata Powers, Wipro, Tata Technology, Defence Stocks, Chemical Stocks which are monopoly sort of or wire and cable stocks such as Polycab – and so on.

So, the importance of two separate demat accounts with different brokers may be useful for many reasons. One such is that your free shares are kept there and may give you extraordinary profits in times to come.

Secondly, at times exchanges do not allow sale and purchase of shares at the same time or the same day. So, one can buy here and sell on another demat account. Only after checking legality thereof. It is better to have a different account in a different name such as that of your spouse.

There may be other advantages which may be there and time will help us to make use of them.

7. Selection of Shares

Number of shares and amount of investment

Let's understand first that any amount of investment in shares is a penny as the market is so wide and big that any amount of money you may have, is just insignificant.

Yes, it may be enough to give a ripple effect to penny stocks or mid cap stocks... And for that one needs to understand and apprehend from various signals they give. To know them or to guess them is not a child's play rather is an art, which takes time to understand and the dog-like smelling power is developed over a period with experience. Once that happens one gets a signal in advance.

Just a few animals sense the coming of an earthquake and start shouting or running.

It will take time and is a must know thing to insulate yourself from greed and as such must take steps to go through the tests discussed in a separate chapter.

Which stocks we need to have in our portfolio needs special study. Some argue that we should not have more than 25 stocks in our portfolio – (I have 260 + stocks in my portfolio – reduced from 320 plus). Now, I want to reduce them to 100 and later on to 25 or so.

Warren Buffet has said that one should not have more than 12 stocks under one's portfolio.

Need discussion on the same … to form an opinion as to what to do? And what is your take on this?

The share market is sea and any amount of investment is less. Therefore, one needs to follow a strict discipline approach as big sharks are there to help you lose money without you realizing and the moment you realise, it will be too late.

The road is perilous- one needs careful treading – keeping watch for greed- sharks- experts who are on the lookout for skimming out cream from your-these traits and before you realise, it will be too late, besides beyond your imagination or understanding.

Sensible investors shall follow that road half way through, and take a u turn and follow the road which is clear and thus reach the goal quickly before others join. One can follow a similar pattern after studying and testing the road following the parameters discussed in this chapter.

What one needs is not to follow the greed within, rather must keep yourself away from the same under all circumstances. As greed suppresses rational thinking, the mind gets usurped where one cannot think logically, as one is under the mystic power of greed.

Our goal must be big but small careful steps should be taken to achieve them. A thousand-mile journey starts with just one little step.

The other aspect is emotional decision, tossing away logic and deciding in a sentimental situation. At times however, gut feeling can be more rewarding than logical thinking for the simple reason that when news is spread that the USA has instead of cutting interest rates, the market shall tumble down unexpectedly beyond imagination world-wide, maybe temporarily. For the news has as such nothing to do with the companies which are strong enough from all angles and thus falling of the whole market from large caps to medium and small ones has nothing to do largely. But it happens and destroys many weak hearted people who are playing on borrowed money or exceeding their risk capability beyond a certain limit and are forced to dispose of the portfolio or are helpless but have to watch their wealth eroding helplessly before their eyes.

The catastrophe has to end somewhere and when it stops, most of the traders have already burnt their money and are clueless about how it all happened and at this stage post-mortem has no value whatsoever. Except a lesson which is costly, no doubt but that is your investment provided you have not run away from the arena whose parameters you ignored and punishment is but an automatic outcome. Remember Krishna the God who says every karma has a corresponding effect.

One forgets, that after a while, everything has to fall in place and becomes favourable with time by the overall share index going up and up under all circumstances, especially in a developing economy like ours.

Patience is the name of the game. Playing with your own money is an insulation against substantial loss, if any occurring, when the chips are down, provided one has abundance of patience and with experience becomes immune to ups and downs knowingly that the bad phase shall pass. Rather, if one has money in fixed instruments, breaking them now and buying under the falling market under these circumstances can result in excellent rewards in the short-term.

8. Is the management playing positively with its stake in a company in a business-like manner or otherwise?

This has special significance and must be considered while making investment decisions.

If the management is increasing its stake in the company? Reason thereof

If the management is decreasing its stake in the company? Why and reason thereof.

If the management pledges its shares for expansion – for squaring off loan or directors selling its stake for personal reasons?

These matters or this type of information has special significance for the growth of the company or fate of the company. Needs special thinking in order to evaluate your decision.

Similarly, when a company is de-pledging its shares, it must be rewarded in a positive manner and that will result in demand for shares after considering other factors … Case in point is that of Suzlon and now Reliance Power going to free their shares while investing or reducing stake or increasing stake in the company or to get out completely from such investment.

Let's remember it is an investment and not a love affair, a single or couple of shares should not become our passion or love affair so that we forget the original purpose why we are in the stock market?

For instance, consider the recent case of Reliance Power. Just as the company's fortunes were about to turn positive, news broke that Anil Ambani had been penalized by SEBI for misusing his authority and diverting company funds. Consequently, the company's shares plummeted, hitting lower circuits daily for four consecutive days. This highlights the importance of diversification, demonstrating that reliance on a single stock can be perilous.

9. Share market as a God given opportunity

We are dealing here with the share market – however we must not forget that in this century and coming decades the number of opportunities which are going to present before us are like the number of stars in the sky.

❖ Any segment you choose you can with discipline achieve multimillionaire status for sure.

❖ What we all need basically is, to do our homework sincerely– with discipline, integrity, passion, unwavering faith in our vision, guiding philosophy being, how can I create opportunity for my friends, colleagues, customers? or a person who approaches for guidance. How could my expertise/ knowledge be of assistance and at least not to harm anyone's interest?

How much return are we targeting? And in how much time? And thus, we need to go on booking the profit partially in any case.

We need to remember that most shares shall see the pattern of rise and fall and with time we shall through our experience or gut feeling, as the time passes, shall be aware of such tides and can thus decide to offload partially and add, on every fall so that without affecting the portfolio we add to our income to enjoy and cherish side by side.

"The longer you wait for a losing trade to reverse and go in your favor, the greater the likelihood that you are on the wrong side of a trend."

–Steve Burns

10. Balanced strategy for selection of stock from a particular segment

All of us have limited resources and most of us after hearing the experts on TV that so and so share is likely to rise in so much period and has the potential to double in so much time or so.

The particular share has gone down by 40% to 50% and is the right time to enter. Most of the investors are likely to invest whatever they could. Always expecting a stock rally.

With the result the number of stocks increases and the profit from few stocks squares off with losses from other stocks.

Thinking only if he had invested in a particular stock he would have made money.

Under these circumstances one is carrying luggage of more stocks and one is confused about which ones to carry on and which ones to leave? For this purpose, I follow the following principle in arriving at the selection of a few best out of five or six in the same category.

For instance, in financial stocks such as Bajaj Finance, Reliance Jio, IREDA, RITES, IRFC, Power Finance Corporation and so on.

Name	Current price	Expected price	% Increase
	10.09.2024	10.09.2026	
Reliance	3000	4300	65
Reliance Jio financial services	351	1050	200

RVNL	565	1130	100
IRFC	170	510	200
IREDA	230	690	200
SYNFORM	26	78	200
TATA Technology	1091	2200	100
SUZLON	78	330	300
TATA Motors	1035	2600	150
HAL	4685	9300	100
Paradeep Defence	1180	2800	150
Infibeam Avenue	30	90	200

So, by preparing the above statements and using our own best judgement, one can decide how much to allocate one's investment, in which share and know by that time the expected result.

It should not be far away on total somehow. This will add to one's experience and approval of method to a large extent. Only time will prove our hindsight against the unpredictable market.

This way, one can create an imaginary picture considering various factors and parameters: news, profit and loss, etc., and make your own chart to compare. All of us shall have our own and shall differ in practice but since we need to use our own mind, therefore to compute we need to weigh the data and come to some estimate. Only time will tell who is right, as there are millions of permutations and combinations to give us direction. For many other unknown incidents can change the whole game. This will help us proceed in an indicative direction and decide. To my mind the best bet should be Reliance, JIO and IRFC but opinions can differ. So, I shall be betting on these two in a major way in this sector.

A similar exercise can be undertaken in case of chemical stocks – IT stocks- and further divide the stocks in large cap, mid cap and small cap according to our risk appetite.

All of us can have various parameters to decide our own way–however one must keep consideration of the overall picture and various ratios – as has been described either directly in the book or indirectly for guidance.

I have found the finance sector has given me healthy returns and better than any other sector. Same way due to the cyclical nature of stocks it is possible it is now the turn of chemical stocks to offer opportunity to make a killing.

In times to come AI stocks can deliver unimaginable returns. Even defence stocks or related ones may give more than the index returns in general.

Decision is yours and risk is yours. So, one can choose a couple of stocks from each category and see the magic happening.

11. Loan Availed and Interest Whether being Paid in Time and Coverage thereof

Companies do avail loans and are necessitated for many reasons. Companies with zero debt are always preferred and get super ratings, such as Infosys, TCS, Tata Technology and many more.

There are industries where capital infusion has to be on large scale and debt burden in case of delay in projects or cost inflation of the input is volatile thus affecting the profitability of the company. In such cases one has to evaluate the company on a different parameter. One key indication shall be long term feasibility and demand scenario. Such as coal based electric generation companies. An example is Jaiprakash Power or Reliance Power.

Loan has to be availed as the same is capitalised as such power plants take time to implement and start generating electricity. The major reason for default in repayment arises because of escalation of cost of input and extra time taken to start operations.

Government policy besides environment clarences as the world is moving towards carbon free usage of materials.

Mismanagement – lack of experience- government policy- cost of input and such other things can cause disruptions in the feasibility of the project and thus profitability.

Loan has to be availed in case of NBFC companies where they have to lend and more loans availed, more shall be profitability of the companies. Cases of the same are Bajaj Finance – Jio Finance- IRFC-IREDA- RITES- and many others.

In this competitive environment where scope is also enormous and in India it has just begun.

If we compare in India only, around 3-4% of people invest in the share market, whereas in China the percentage is 30% plus and in the USA it is 55% of the population which is investing in the equity market. These figures can give indication as to coming opportunities in the Indian stock market and its allied industries such as brokerage firms.

In crux, we have to see if the company is paying its interest without default and in time the indication can be taken as a positive one.

This aspect gains importance while considering investing as one has to see how much is a company's income or profit, which can cover interest with sufficient margin. A high rate of interest except in case of finance companies- had an adverse impact on profitability. Therefore, zero debt companies show more profits and reward shareholders with handsome returns. Case in point can be that of Nestle- Gillette.

Companies do avail loans and are necessitated for many reasons. However, in due course of time the measure one has to see that out of gross income the servicing of interest is not only being served or how many times the same can be served. For instance, if the loan is 100 cr. The principle to be paid every year is 10 cr, and interest too is 1% of the principle. The same is paid in time and the margin is such that it is possible to serve it many times in case of emergency. So, the real test is it being paid easily out of extra income and reserves are more than the loan. Coupled with the same both must be taken into account before deciding to invest in such a share for safety parameters. However, many more parameters also cannot be ignored side by side.

12. Raising funds for the company – either by way of loan or through bonds- FDI and so on has generally a positive effect on the share prices of the company.

There are many cases when companies borrow or get investments from the market or some big investors – the effect in the market is positive and prices start rising for the simple reasons

a) Interest burden is going to come down – thus increasing the profitability in the coming quarters.

b) Expansion is going to take or capacity is going to increase – resulting in more profits in the coming years.

c) The investor must have studied the project and thus already ground work as to feasibility is supposed to have been undertaken and thus is a signal for investing.

d) Credit rating is awarded and is raised higher than before is another sign of the strength of the company.

e) Some big existing players known for its management competence, quality invested in the company say, 10% or more is another indication as to its turnaround possibility.

f) Or some new innovation has been developed by the company which can create a sea change in input-cost. A recent example is of the company launching sodium powered batteries which will cost 5 times less in the market.

As such there can be many more reasons and the same can be interpreted accordingly in order to take a call to enhance one's stake in the company.

> *"I have found that, when the market is going down, you buy funds wisely. At some point in the future, you will be happy. You won't get there – by reading. Now is the only time to buy."*
>
> **–Peter Lynch**

Importance of management stake is a major parameter to consider in almost all the cases barring few. Those cases which are exceptions shall be dealt with separately.

When the stake of the management is large enough it shows management has passion and confidence. Sure, of their vision to the scope, that is why in the first place they started this business. 50% and more of its stake speaks volume about the management

In case the stake goes up to 75% all the better. In most of the cases unless it is capital intensive or it is a government company, the said stake may be more than even 75%. However as "per the rules, those" companies who have more than 75% shares have to dilute excess within three years or five years maximum, to bring down to 75% maximum.

So, the investor has to consider while placing its trust and continue selection of such shares that the stake may be diluted and for the time being it may come down or may be under the grip of bears.

This especially applies to those investors who are traders and whose goal is to make some quick gain and not for those who are long term investors and wealth creators.

Companies having 50% stake and increasing the same is a good sign for the investors for who knows more about the inside of the company more than investors himself or themselves?

Similarly, when the promoters are reducing their stake is a warning sign for the investors and if the trend persists a red flag, and earlier the investors sell better it is.

13. Government Policy: Is It Encouraging?

Backing of the government is not only necessary but the soul of any company for its general progress.

As of today, our present Government is working overtime to see:

a) Infrastructure development on large scale as it knows it is mandatory for the country

1) Be it transport – which includes railways, shipping, air travel, ports, freight corridor, road transport, logistics, tourism, and so on
2) Be it energy, coal, wind, thermal, nuclear, and so on
3) Be it education, medical, engineering, AI, digital
4) Employment generation – through all the above initiatives
5) 'Make in India' initiative which has given great boost to Indian companies and thus going to serve in multiple ways – such as greater employment – greater exports- less dependence on imports – saving on foreign exchange- exposure to our population and skilled workers is an opportunity on a scale unheard before.
6) One type of education throughout the country – one constitution - one nation theory and thus opening of IITs, medical colleges; promoting education ... to one and all. Opening of many educational institutions or encouragement to local artisans – and all this is being taken care of not only in particular pockets but in every district possible.

7) Country's Sanatan Sanskriti by restoring the old values which have been based on logic and have been ignored for many centuries – which is helping generate not only tourism but creating unthinkable number of jobs – creating value to the population a huge source of extra income and thus raising their standard of living.

8) Foreign policy and invitation to big companies to make investment in India by creating values and one window clearances and thus doubly benefiting the country in multiple ways.

b) Government understands that real growth of the country can take place only if the whole population is taken into account and it should be inclusive growth and not exclusive.

c) By making it digitally possible for the whole population to benefit and making sure that the amount through which the government wishes to help the ordinary farmer, women, the girls who should be in school by sending them money directly to their account. Thus, removing the barrier of chipping away a major chunk of money in between as it used to happen and only 15% hardly used to reach the real beneficiary – which is not the case now.

d) Understanding the difficulties of the poor people by providing them shelter – bathroom facilities – no government could ever think of ... and thus caring for the population of the country without looking at caste or creed.

e) The government recognises its responsibility to serve the people, being of the people, by the people, and for the people.

In nutshell, it is the broader framework and vision which is helping grow the market to its capacity when the overall status of one and all is increasing and average income or to say per capita income of the larger part of population is increasing, thus in no time tsunami is going to take place in the stock market, quantum jump of which can hardly be imagined right now.

There is an indication already to this effect from the following few figures if we care to analyse properly.

1. Per month SIP figures are increasing
2. Number of trading accounts are increasing considerably
3. Middle class where both husband and wives are earning are increasing magically
4. Savings in fixed deposits/ mutual Funds are also increasing substantially
5. By increasing the number of households above poverty line the demand for white goods, two wheelers – four wheelers etc. is increasing in double figures

All this is going to go on doubling our industry growth tremendously in the coming years and shall have a multiplier effect on a large part of the economy. ***Thus, making rich all those in share market who will be using the opportunity by understanding the principles and basic parameters discussed in the book – thereby making use of the book written for you and you only.***

For investors in share market: A lesson or clue

Overall development is in place and one can see the future is bright and thus opportunities are great overall and the need of the hour is to invest in growing companies by properly analysing the pros and cons and by using the gut feeling. The next twenty years are going to be a time to harvest money left and right. Yes, due diligence is required and that too by using common sense and keeping away from the – get-rich-quickly mindset. Everything takes time and for some it may take 10 years yet for some life time, as such basic thing is to write down first what exactly you wish to achieve? It is there before our eyes – we need to follow the principles described in this book without casting doubt but using ditto and with common sense.

"Volatility in the up direction is not a problem, it's only downward volatility that offers discourse."

– Coreen T. Sol

Conclusion

Demand as such for shares of any company worth its name either by performance or management's reputation besides those companies which are going to come up with IPOs is going to see an explosive growth as the number of investors who are going to enter the stock market shall create a Tsunami and thus market is going to go up and up only … many opportunities shall COME our way to go ON booking profits in each and every company by buying when down and selling when up …. With experience only, one shall have that intuition or perception to know or by exploring the parameters explained in this book along with.

You are lucky to be going through this book… and shall be rewarded for sure.

"The way to make money is to buy when blood is running in the streets."

– John D Rockefeller

14. Market Share of the Company—Domestic or International

(This aspect has to be weighed properly and the effect it shall have on the profitability of the company keeping in view costing vs. production and utilization of capacity of the plant expansion scope and time to double the capacity or a particular target time it will take and latest technology if any in relation to that product.)

Companies are known at times by brand names. Such as Nestle, Colgate, Pidilite, Tata Motors, Maruti, Ambuja Cement, and so on.

Companies generally have an international presence – Coca Cola, Pepsi, Gillette, and so on... their strategy has been unique and functional.

Very few examples are there when already the market is being served by competent companies and the best example is that of Airtel and Vodafone. When Reliance entered, surprising the market and today it has more than 35% share of the market with its strategy to enter the market in its own unique way… unsettling the whole market thus making few companies exit the market unwillingly but sensibly.

Like Gillette very cleverly making people addicted to this type of shaving with their fancy quality product and thus raising prices on every opportunity where the consumer is helpless but to use the same product as he has become accustomed to that particular type of product only.

Such companies are safe and one can invest in these companies without much thinking – although the return may be meager but at times can give huge dividends over a long period of time.

Their market share is not only huge but massive and generally any new entrant has to think 100 times before entering in these areas unless and until having not only deep pockets but come out with a new innovative product which can beat the existing one with its unique additional benefits.

Case in point is Hindustan Aeronautics – making planes with the support of government backing and is a sort of monopoly.

Case in point is Reliance Refinery which is one of the largest in Asia and not many companies can think of starting such a massive refining capacity as it requires billions of Dollars…

In the same way companies, which have large scale production capacity – a name such as Pidilite- industries known best for its product Fevicol, a household name.

A company having major share and with good management with zero debt is a right candidate for investment when available at a discount... one has to keep watch as to 52-week high and low and history of the price movement for the last couple of years which will give indication and without doubt one has to keep in view the cyclical nature of the stock as well.

For instance, every segment has its time in a cycle of 3-7 years depending upon its product and international scene.

For example, the chemical sector is down for many reasons and the major one is change in petrol prices. The moment crude prices take a turn, demand for its products shall rise and thus the time to reap profits shall fall in your lap but for that one needs to invest now in stocks such as Aarti Industries – Pidilite- and many others lying subdued right now.

In the same way one needs to understand that demand of cold drinks shall fall in winter season so that third quarter result shall be lower profits and in summer when cold drinks and ice-cream demand increases the quarter next results shall be much better which will see rise in share prices and generally an opportunity to buy before the results are out. Keeping this into consideration share prices of Varun Beverages are likely to go up after June results.

Here it is important to understand the share market is akin to the human body where each part has its role and no individual part can be given less importance. To grasp the contribution of every part of the body is important and therefore to understand the share market one needs to weigh every news- performance, government policy, demand and supply, company's health, management, level playing field, happiness quotient of the employees and so on. There are a multitude of factors one can never even fathom.

Here are some shares compared to body organs, highlighting their qualities, values, or traits:

1. Heart Shares - Like HDFC Bank, pumps life into the economy, steady and reliable.
2. Brain Shares - Like TCS, intelligent and innovative, thinking ahead.
3. Eye Shares - Like Infosys, clear vision, focused growth.
4. Ear Shares - Like Zee Entertainment, listening to the market, tuning into trends.
5. Hand Shares - Like L&T, skilled and crafty, building strong foundations.
6. Liver Shares - Like Hindustan Zinc, purifying and refining, growth through challenges.
7. Kidney Shares - Like Britannia Industries, filtering and balancing, consistent performance.
8. Lung Shares - Like ITC, breathing life into the market, steady growth.
9. Stomach Shares - Like Jubilant Food Works, digesting and absorbing, growing through challenges.
10. Muscle Shares - Like Tata Motors, strong and resilient, flexing through market fluctuations
11. Skin Shares - Like Maruti Suzuki, adaptable and protective, navigating market changes.
12. Bone Shares - Like JSW Steel, strong and supportive, foundational growth.
13. Nerve Shares - Like HUL, sensitive and responsive, quick to adapt.

This is a good way to relate to the shares as to its qualities and thus can help identify to add to portfolios depending upon one's risk appetite.

15. Value Unlocking

Merger-demerger

Case in point is that of Jio finance and Tata motors – Tata investment – Vedanta.

Knowledge of expected merger or de-merger in most of the cases can unlock value of companies beyond our estimate or expectation.

Therefore, one can decide in advance as to start investing in these shares and when that happens one can reap the benefit of the same to a large extent.

This can be done by creating the comparison after expected demerger of companies and evaluating the segments PE of merged or de-merged entities afterwards and looking at them by comparing the PE of similar companies in the same field.

For instance, let's take the case in point, that of Tata Motors – where the passenger vehicle segment is likely to be separated from that of commercial vehicles. The demerged entities are compared to Ashoka Leyland and in case of Passenger-Cars to be compared with Maruti.

Similarly, we need to share the case of Jio Finance with Bajaj finance and others.

> *"But what actually registers in the stock market's fluctuations are not the events themselves, but the human reactions to these events. In short, how millions of individual men and women feel these happenings may affect their future."*
>
> **–Bernard Baruch**

16. Demand and Overall Expected Growth of the Industry

Client Base of the Company

All this is important and we need to be aware as to expected growth of the industry keeping in view the Government Policy as well as global efforts as to reach zero carbon policy of the world organization for the good of the planet and signatories of the same and promise made thereof.

Electric vehicles battery—lithium or sodium-based ones or any new development in the industry which may arise.

India is fast moving towards new avenues to see that dependence on petrol is reduced to the minimum possible and encouragement to ethanol-based fuel is given push as never before.

These aspects can be taken into consideration while making investment decisions in companies which may be entering in these fields after researching and studying various companies and comparing them as to various factors as are mentioned in the parameters. Your quick action can give excellent returns provided your portfolio is well balanced and all eggs are not put in one basket.

Major companies may be from railways, ship building, aerospace, planes, freight, infrastructure and so on.

17. Order book of the company

Order book is large enough to last for many years at current capacity. Because of its quality, the company gets repeat orders.

Another point being the company is capable of executing orders in time, which adds to its trust and dependability in domestic as well as in international arena.

Case in point is that of L & T, HAL. Suzlon and Engineers India ltd.

In case of manufacturing companies such as of Asian Paints, Indigo Paints, Pidilite Industries where these companies are putting up additional plants to increase their capacities, keeping into consideration extra demand they are experiencing foreseeing and for another reason to up-grade the new technology in its operations besides future demand and change of robotics entry along with AI and digital economy replacing fast the existing way of operations to compete in future.

18. Financials of the company

This aspect is very wide and the more we delve on it, the less it is.

When a penny is coming – welcome it with both hands – respect it – when the penny is leaving stop it and see it does not leave your door…. This is an art – as well as science. Learn it. In college we read it "that money is a means to an end and not an end in itself."

It is very complicated as well as simple depending upon our grasp of the figures and deductions.

One can interpret the same thing in different manner depending upon education and understanding of the economic parameters.

For instance, India is taking out loans and the amount has gone up considerably. Why and is it too big an amount? Actually, it is nothing compared to our GDP. We need to evaluate the growth of the economy and overall prosperity of the common man and the reach of various schemes to the last deserving and needy person or family to the last point anywhere in the country.

Without understanding the core pain which is inclusive growth on which our prime minister is working upon diligently.

Inclusive growth means as long as the poorest of the poor is brought to the main stream of the national growth and gets the benefit there is no use of any growth. Basic necessities have to be met under all circumstances, that is Roti, Kapda and Makaan. Not only this, our government is taking care of electricity- water-education – employment generation on village level too.

The progress of the country is incomplete without the economic growth of one and all. Once people say 100% are given shelter and food and/ or opportunities the demand shall boost like never before and shall result in economic boom rather than Tsunami in economic growth of the nation. That is the only way when we shall be reaching the 3rd economy by 2027 and shall be almost on equal footing of the most developed nations.

All these need to be considered besides following to evaluate the company's horoscope to decide to invest in any company to get the best results in terms of profits for self. FMCG companies can bring great bonanza for the investors in the coming years and decades.

On an individual basis, besides worrying for the nation- if we try to look after our family and its economic growth the value shall automatically reach the whole nation and thus prosperity … for one and all shall ensue.

While deciding to invest in any company understanding of the financials is the core which will help us decide better: such as

a) Profit for the last three years
b) Sales growth for the last three years
c) Dividend history
d) Bonus history
e) Seasonal effect examples such as coca cola, paint industry so the quarterly results shall be different for different companies and as such relevant factors must be considered to compare the results.

f) Windfall profits: that is abnormal gains such as sale of some part of the unit or disposing of some nonprofit making units etc.

g) Rise in prices of consumable inputs- or fall or rise in prices of input materials such as minerals and metal stocks can affect the profit of the company considerably.

h) Research and development – a new product is developed or new technology is introduced with the result the margin increases and thus the profitability of the company.

i) Large orders are received and are consistent for a long time.

j) Ratios, beta cost of sales

k) Taxes- subsidies – export incentives

l) Import ban – export ban (case in point is that of computers) Rice export ban so that local prices may not go up

As such, there can be very many pointers in financials and each one shall have its own impact in a different manner.

However, all this can fly out of the window due to any one of the external factors in no time. For example, all is going perfectly fine and one fine morning we find that the world is at world-war stage at any moment. People would start hoarding food items like never before and demand of all items shall surge abruptly when business community shall see an opportunity to start hoarding of the food grains etc. and thus add to the existing demand further with the result the prices of shares may have effect on the FMCG companies temporarily by upper circuit for couple of days.

Consequently, after the honeymoon is over, the fall shall ensue automatically and those who have entered the market at a much later stage, shall bear the brunt.

In the same way demand and supply which is seasonal, affects the share prices – for instance, gold prices surge especially during marriage season and Diwali season.

Cold-drink companies demand surges during summer and go to the lower side by winter season.

Same is the case with ice-cream.

All the above pointers of financial parameters can be discussed in detail but will make it more complicated, therefore, the best way is to have a little bit of indicative knowledge as we are not going to do masters in this subject. Masters we will be, through our experience in times to come, if we follow parameters seriously and honestly without greed and impatience. With that, we will not only make handsome profits but shall learn the techniques which great investors use and thus may follow on their footsteps to garner super profits from the share market which is a rare phenomenon.

It is the first million which is difficult to make and once you start making profit you shall be encouraged to make rational decisions and the rule of compounding shall make you rich beyond your own imagination. **Patience, discipline and control over greed is the only way out.**

There can be exceptions to this rule depending upon the industry to industry and that point has to be considered. For if the company is running in losses and has large debt, but now it has started making profit and its liability is being reduced one way or the other, that shall make a lot of difference and change the whole game of awarding points.

These things have to be considered on broader parameters on a case-to-case basis, before we take a call to buy a particular stock.

In the case of an NBFC company the liability has a significance in a different manner. More the loan, more may be profits and thus need to calculate the liability of the company under a different light under a different lens.

19. Performance, Price and Tragedies

When performance is above average, the price too shall be above average when the performance is sterling one, the price too shall be of diamond. When the performance is down the price tends to go down little more as a percentage of when it was rising and thus in case it is seasonal or temporary rise or fall, because of external factors. That means the opportunity to invest when out of season because the prices tend to be lower. And here one needs to go through various parameters to arrive at the sane and appropriate conclusion to invest or not?

For if certain shares are rising say by thousands of percentage points and few of those who have bought at the peak may feel the heat if some grave incident happens be it government policy, fight among directors, abrupt change in technology or whole plant being destroyed in a natural disaster like earthquake, big fire or a cyclone. Or some fraud or money laundering case like those of Choksi- Neerav Modi or Vijay Mallya.

20. Time Matters

All shares have one common denominator and that is, it has a head and tail like a coin.

When you buy it matters.

The same share can make you rich and give you handsome gains and the same can ruin your dream too. Timely entry matters and gains importance. Depends upon the share and its journey.

There are plenty of examples: (copied from WhatsApp)

i) Tata Motors: Destroyed wealth by 90% during 2015-2020 and generated 1200% return during 2020-2024

ii) ITC-Destroyed wealth by 50% during 2017-2020 but generated 180% return during 2020-2024

iii) Suzlon-Destroyed wealth by 99% during 2008-2023- but generated 400% return during 2023-2024

iv) Titagarh Rail: Destroyed wealth by 80% during 2008-2020 but generated 4100% return during 2020-2024

v) Kotak Bank-Generated 70,000% return during 2001-2020 but no returns between 2020-2024

vi) Bank of Baroda-Destroyed wealth by 80% during 2010-2020 but generated 450% return during 2020-2024

vii) Jubilant Food-Generated 3700% return during 2010-2021 but destroyed wealth by 40% during 2021-2024

viii) India bulls Housing Finance-Generated 500% return during 2014-2018 BUT Destroyed wealth by 95% during 2018-2023

Generated 100% return during 2023-24

It is for sure that the same thing is happening even now, and we may not be aware of it!

Those who can smell this and identify the sleeping giants hidden in the form of penny stocks or otherwise, in a particular sector - or in future segment shares can definitely make a killing. This requires out of the box research with keen penetrating eyes to dig the diamond like finding a pin from the sea floor. Your idea, patience, knowledge, experience, use of technology, help from experts to locate the same from the sea-bed through laser, magnetic innovation or existing technology may assist in finding the same.

Nothing is impossible- the only thing is we must know where we are searching and is it worth investing that much?

I recall in SRCC, our auditing lecturer gave us a good lesson: while auditing, invest your time in checking 10% of vouchers which account for 90% in value and leave 90% which have 10% value in terms of money. This learning saves lots of time in the future in our lives practically in every aspect.

Time is of essence: some of us try to do too much analysis and while doing so, the opportunity slips from our hand. Too much analysis brings paralysis.

CAUTION: At times we set out to find the gold in Africa and come back empty handed and to our surprise we had left the venue which belonged to us was a gold mine itself.

Case in point is in most of the cases a number of people who go out of India to make money end up as a lower income group because life nowhere is so easy. This is the case of most uneducated people who leave for Canada by selling their golden land in Punjab and work there in foreign countries as labourers or masons or drivers or delivery boys. So, in the same way some stocks may lay dumb for quite some time and at the most unexpected time erupts like a volcano. Art is required to identify volcanoes like stocks. Years of experience may come handy.

"A winning strategy must include losing."

– from Rich Dad and Poor Dad

21. Resources in Hand or Dependability

For expansion and for creating value of the product to raise the demand of some usefulness of the innovation, branding is a must. Brands sell and for that it takes years at times or deep pockets.

Colgate – when we talk of it, all of us relate it to toothpaste

Coca-Cola when we say all of us relate it to cold drinks and is the most preferred one for most. People have been drinking since my school days as we used to get a coupon of one anna or small bottles of Coca Cola and they were pretty attractive.

When Reliance Jio was launched, it offered free usage for some time and in a record time of 73 days it created 100 million subscribers – a world record. Only because of the conviction of the management as to usage of data – speed of data and deep pockets. It was not only a mind-game, it was value for money too.

Why does one do business? Only to make money and that is where good profitability comes down to play a significant role and consistency is even more important.

These companies move like African elephants and mow down their competition remarkably well and gain market share in a big way.

At times they become blue whales too, eating small companies in a big way to save time and creating win-win situations for one and all.

22. International Rating Agencies – Local Ones

This is another material indication which can help to some extent as to showing direction in the coming days. If the rating has gone up it shall be taken in good stead and if the same is downgraded the effect will be negative obviously.

23. Federal rate increase or cuts- RBI rate cuts or increase

All this has lots to do with prices of shares as because of this either way shall result into more investment coming in the share market in case the banks cut interest rates and thus it is expected to result into rise in share index and prices of shares of those companies especially who can expect foreign investment – either institutions or funds management companies.

Federal rate cuts can have a far-reaching effect on IT shares whose business is in America or European companies.

24. Government policy towards a particular nation or industry

This is also an important indication as there may be threats as to dealing with that country at a particular time. Governments may take steps on withdrawal of concessions or increasing duties on the products or even freezing of account for any flimsy reasons. Case in point is that of Canada now.

25. SEBI – Strictures

SEBI's role in the share market cannot be undermined as the institution has been created for the safety of the investors. Many instructions warnings putting the company under NIFTY or increasing or decreasing the lower circuit or higher circuit does affect the sentiments of the investors. Changing the category also makes a lot of difference and higher the category foreign investment institutions do come forward to invest in their own interest. So, any move positive or negative shall have considerable difference in decision making while taking a call to invest.

26. International Scenario

Anything happening today in the world of business matters a lot, maybe for a short duration. For instance, our relations with Canada are being affected by the deterrent of Canada for their support to the Khalistan agenda by the Sikh community by a few misguided youths.

Even when we came in support of Israel, or for that matter neutral in case of the Ukraine episode, most of the countries of the world were not liking it. Even the USA wanted us to denounce Russia for the same. However, our foreign policy is to be independent and to have good relations with all the countries in equal measure, and in the best interest of the country.

27. Market of USA, Europe, Japan and Few Others

Today we are part of a global village comprising around 800 crores of people or say 8 billion across 195 or so countries. Any news in any corner of the world reaches us in seconds.

Today the information is available on Google and many other search engines which work 24/7 and the volume of information is exploding like never before.

Yes, it has its advantages and disadvantages. Just akin to nuclear bomb either we can produce electricity or use it for destruction purposes. Similar is the case regarding use of valuable and mass volume of information and its source matters.

One biased piece of information with an intention to kill a company can be effective in a wrong way. Latest example is that of the Hindenburg Report against Adani with a deep conspiracy not against the company but against our nation it seems.

So, filtration of the same, gains importance beyond doubt.

For instance, if there is by chance information that a super power has decided to nuke a particular nation and in retaliating on the same if the wrong button is pressed without verifying there could be holocaust outcome. Even to imagine the consequences shall create goosebumps.

Therefore, as a smart investor one needs to develop an art to filter the information to come to the right conclusion to decide the investment strategy.

Investors have to develop the instinct to be active and awake all the 24 hours of the day. Like I was going through news that an investor got himself registered as a broker in Switzerland, so as to take advantage of buying there and selling in New York as the time difference is so much that by the time New York exchange opens, he can buy or sell there to take advantage of the difference of prices. A genius of an idea. So once again it suggests time and again that it is smart work which counts.

One cannot ignore temporary effects such as the rise or fall of Nasdaq- NIKKIE, or DAX of German or for that matter Shanghai stock exchange HKEX exchanges share prices which shall have repercussions on the prices of Indian exchanges generally in a remarkable manner.

28. Change in Technology

This has a new meaning in the context of our changing scenario of world trade and fast technical innovative changes it is bringing daily on a mass scale where a small innovation can bring sea change in the profitability of the company and those companies which ignore the same can disappear from the scene faster than one can think.

From steam engine to electric, our railways have seen tremendous changes and now solar, and new and economic fuels in the shape of ethanol, etc. the solar panels being deployed on the railway tracks to reduce the cost of land and space has another advantage as well and thus keeping pace with latest technology has its empirical effect on the use of such latest AI technology in order to survive in the fast competitive world, where cut throat competition is the norm especially when the world has become flat. That leads us to our next important development called Artificial intelligence and robotic technology.

It is propagated that there is nothing like Artificial Intelligence—it should be called Different Intelligence.

29. AI-Digital Economy

In today's world-economy, all those who can show promise of honey – will automatically attract business their own way. As the flies do come from nowhere when they smell the same.

In the same way, the growing demand for all the products in India is rising on a massive scale with the exceptional growth of 8-9% every year beating most countries and it seems is going to last for the next three decades for sure. Who and which country can ignore this huge market?

Today our country's all-time growth is gaining unimaginable proportions and as our government vision is clear and economic sense is to see development of all sectors in a big way with a clear understanding of inclusive growth as a core mantra.

No country or company can survive today without the use of AI and digital payment systems and it seems in the coming years the printing of currency shall be history.

So, these technical developments being opted by a company sooner than the competition, shall bear great impact on the profitability of the company and be a point for investment decisions by the investors to a large extent.

This field has just been in the offing and has tremendous potential in the coming years in all our daily activities in one or the other way.

Chat GPT and like it so many new innovations are making us addicted to these gadgets with its pros and cons like any new product.

The next generation has a great future, however provided one can balance one's time use in a profitable manner positively. Otherwise, the danger of these tools can be detrimental to one's career and thus the role of parents is going to be much more important in how they guide their children psychologically.

Gaming is one such thing in today's education context where most of our young children are becoming addicted to the same, which is going to be a big hurdle in their career.

This is a paradox, that most of us are consuming foods which are not good for health and still the same is being promoted by companies and the government is not taking any steps for them to get tremendous revenue. The case in point is that of cold drinks-liquor and whisky companies, even sweets which have gained a lot in the recent years with self-life extended because of preservatives and chemicals use, thus a nonproductive thing for the nation's health programs.

Investors have the right to profit no doubt, but have social responsibility too in the interest of our next generation and national economy. Balance has to be maintained and through education this must be handled in the overall interest of the nation and its population.

These things largely shall help the investor to decide and act accordingly and avoid such investments where the short-term gain results in long term loss.

Few readers may feel that this book is for making millions and this topic has nothing to do with it and we are not here to get moral education. So dear readers there is no use of having money which is robbing our education system and spoiling our children as our children are our future and good Sanskar shall help the country in a big manner in all directions ONLY if we care and act in the overall interest of one and all from today itself.

All of us have a great responsibility. The next parameter is connected to it...

30. Integrity – Moral Turpitude

When the company cares for its shareholders and all who in one way or another are related to this mission to educate and learn to become millionaires many times over, there is no use earning and amassing wealth which is not being used for the welfare of the general public.

The TATAs are known for this trait and are respected business groups all over the world.

All investors have made good money from its shares. The group cares for its employees and vendors. Besides, they work not only for profit but all their actions are in the interest of the nation too.

Their integrity is beyond any shade of doubt and that is why investors look forward to their IPOs with great hope and consider investing in the shares of this group because of its integrity which they have developed since the previous century.

There are more than 125 companies under the Tata's brand name directly or indirectly, all work on this theme only. So, the investors have faith and that is why their face value and name Tata has a goodwill few in the world can match.

31. Zero Carbon

As per latest international organization and efforts by all the countries to go zero carbon policy while creating infrastructure in the energy sector.

Zero net carbon policy means to reduce global warming to 1.5°C. Warming of the world which shall reach 1.5°C should be neutralized.

Net zero is an ideal state where the amount of greenhouse gasses (GHGs) released into the earth's atmosphere is balanced by the amount of GHGs removed. Decarbonisation efforts are needed to reach net zero.

Keeping global warming to 1.5°C above pre industrial levels by limiting the buildup of atmospheric GHGs will be necessary to prevent permanent warming of the planet and catastrophic consequences. Those efforts are referred to as decarbonisation. Many companies, countries, and organisations have pledged to decarbonise, or to make the net-zero transition, in the coming years. Power, oil and gas, and transport industries are frequently cited as the biggest emitters, but all industries need to work toward decarbonisation to achieve net zero.

145 countries have decided to participate to galvanize its efforts in reducing carbon and make it a net zero carbon world by 2050 with the support of top multinational companies of the world.

The combined efforts shall open new global opportunities in this new industry by providing new innovative approaches to contribute and all those companies which shall provide such solutions may also get attention of investors alike.

Over-all the share market has to go up and up only. So, I need to select the companies and go on investing -but in between go on booking profits too.

In the context of Indian scenario, no one can deny that the stock market is going to go up and up only, provided we have the present Government whose continuation is a must, for it has blue print, vision, action plan, and will, besides determination to act in their plan for the growth of Indian economy on all fronts. A government which understands the value of infrastructure-inclusive Growth and thus importance of - Sabka Vikas, Sabka Saath and Sabka Pariyas, irrespective of one's caste, creed or religion must be understood holistically from its economic sense.

Without doubt the index is likely to touch 100000 which is hovering around 75000 for quite some time.

Therefore, it is evident that all companies, be they private like those of Adani, Ambani, Munjal's, Mittal's, Mahindra's, Hinduja's and many more shall play not only pivotal roles but deliver to the investor hefty returns in the coming decades.

Even Government companies especially those in the infrastructure – banking and finance – defence are going to deliver more than average return to the shareholders.

When there is all around growth, it results in employment opportunities in an unprecedented manner and in an unexpected way. Besides, all connected and aligned fields too shall develop and result in additional per capita income, thus creating huge demand as a result, domino effect shall ensue, which will create extraordinary results and ultimately bound to be in Favor of intelligent investors – investors who are going to invest on himself by learning the language of successful investors with their experience shall be rewarded handsome returns.

The real bonanza shall be nothing less than a miracle – do you want to be part of those who shall mint money or on the side of those who will only regret the opportunity knowing fully well but indecision and fear of losing money had more weight on their minds.

Jago investors Jago! Come out of your slumber and watch the arrival of golden period in history which will be regarded as the Alladin ka Chirag – Asking you for your wish …and this book which is going to motivate you to be part of this journey in stock market to claim your share – a God given opportunity.

Act or you will be acted upon.

Out of many parameters to go through to identify the stock's worthiness to invest, below are few to look into:

Before we proceed further, lets understand, all this can only give direction and there are many factors which we need to visualise and use the best of judgement to arrive at the most optimum decision.

Gist of these factors broadly:

1. Last three years, growth in profits is more than 15%.
2. Last three years, growth in revenue is more than 15%.
3. Management stake is more than 50%.
4. The Institution's stake is there and is increasing domestic, international or government stake.
5. Price to earn is lower than the industry or very high.

(At times the price is a thousand times price to earning- because the market rewards perception of the management and future scope on count of many parameters. Case of reliance on JIO finance.)

6. Book value.
7. Government policy- positive or encouraging or otherwise.
8. Government import policy or export policy – positive or negative.
9. Beta – if less than 1 is better.
10. Market share of the company.
11. Change in technology expected and chances of outdated technology.

(When the whole industry of internet data was busy in 2G or 3G Mukesh Ambani took the huge risk of bypassing others and initiated 4G and 5G technology)

12. Competition in the industry.
13. Is the company making a turn-around by clearing its huge debts? Case in point is that of Reliance Power, Suzlon and many more.
14. Is the management selling its stake? If yes, why? If increasing its stake – why?
15. Do institutions sell their stake? For profit booking or to know something which a normal investor does not know and cannot know.
16. Is management increasing its stake in the company, which is a good sign.
17. Management's face value – integrity; is it shareholder friendly?
18. Zero carbon mission; strategy and awareness.
19. Is the company adopting the latest technology – keeping pace with the latest norms?
20. What effect it shall have on SEBI's strictures on few companies having similar nature.
21. What is the share of revenue from different countries? Friendly or otherwise and what effect shall have under different situations like war expectation, sanctions by any country if at all.
22. Capacity expansion
23. Raising of resources from different instruments—affect thereof on the market, on profitability in short run or long term.

24. Rating of the company by international agencies or local increasing or decreasing.
25. Sales growth – percentage of market share.
26. Research wing of the company and number of patents registered, especially matters in the pharma industry.
27. AI and digital technology adoption.
28. Where job seekers compete to join the group because of its friendly nature with employees in terms of reputation and facilities.
29. Companies which reward's efficiency – innovation.
30. Value unlocking.
31. Zero debt companies.

There can be as many more things or evolution methods or norms we need to gauge as we go along. Simply put, it is not possible what we are going to encounter in our journey. However, once we start the journey, problems shall be there and solutions also lie in the problem itself so we need to look into it with a positive frame of mind. Believing that every problem has a solution and with that attitude the journey shall be smooth and fruitful.

A warning/caution: No single thing of value can be ignored. It all depends upon how we interpret it. PE matters, but more than that it is the way we analyse. In some cases, PE is thousand times but the profitability expected in the coming years is likely to bring it down to the reasonable valuation. We can see the same in JIO finance and those companies such as Reliance power and Suzlon.

So, our method of diagnosis can differ from company to company keeping in view numerous factors.

"The intelligent investor is a realist who sells to optimists and buys from pessimists."

– Benjamin Graham

❑

11 Pillars of Indian Stock Market

1. Visionary Leadership

Under the visionary ideas and will to implement the same in the interest of the country that has a population of 140 crores plus, our Prime Minister Shri Narendra Damodar Das Modi, who not only knows that infrastructure development of the country is the first priority. In case we wish to help the last person of our population.

2. Bureaucracy

The killer of the Indian economy has been the bureaucratic force of the Indian economy who instead of expediting the growth have been impeding the same with their, know it all thinking.

The same is being dismantled slowly and slowly as it has been eating the economic growth silently for too long.

3. Make in India Initiative

This is not merely a slogan, rather another big initiative from our PM, which is not only boosting the country's growth in terms of GDP as well as saving foreign currency which was going out in a big way. Besides that, exporting our goods, be it in defence, FMCG, IT, AI and boosting railway – ports- energy rather all fields be it roads, education system, tourism – SMEs self-start ups – women-oriented empowering schemes to give them equal opportunity and self-dependent attitude which they truly deserve.

4. Political Career

Most enter politics just for looting money and have nothing to do with the nation's progress as most of these politicians are not only uneducated but have no vision. However, surprisingly mathematics of voting science as to demographic of population division as per caste and other such parameters are known to them like a palm of their hands, for winning the elections- by promising stars to the general public. Unfortunately, the people being down to earth and simple, believe everything they say and regret at leisure.

The present government is aware of these things and working towards real democracy and keeping intact the democratic values. Had it been otherwise no one could utter the nonsense almost all opposition are speaking about.

In larger interest many changes are likely to be introduced to curb the irresponsible statements without justifying the data and mostly unrealistic but biased statements without any solid base knowingly.

5. Inclusive growth is what our government is putting its efforts on a large scale.

The rise of income of weaker sections to lower middle class and thus from middle class to higher income category where both the partners are earning and thus leading to massive growth of white goods, and FMCG goods, propelling growth of the Indian economy to a new-heights. It is only the beginning and with these saving habits increasing in a massive way all around shall make the standard of living rise dramatically.

Following figures shall give us a small glimpse of things to come in the coming decade:

- ❖ Deposits are increasing in government schemes.
- ❖ Mutual funds are getting funds on increasing numbers every quarter
- ❖ Banks are also getting deposits in increasing quantities.
- ❖ Loan disbursals are increasing in a multi-fold way to reach the figure in an unprecedented manner.
- ❖ Number of demat accounts have achieved a new landmark and have reached the figure of 15 crores from 10.5 crores.

6. The stock market has reached the Rs 4 trillion market and within next five years is likely to achieve more than 10 trillion or so. Who is going to benefit?

The 1.5 billion account holders for sure as most of the increase shall find its place in the pockets of those in the stock market, the share capital raised during the same period including premium.

None the less, if we see the figure that 90% of demat holders lose money.

It means 10% shall be the main beneficiaries of the windfall in the stock market.

7. Educational Institutions in Private Sector

Marketing companies—Chat GPT, Microsoft languages, various training centres for imparting NEET tests, English speaking IAS, IPS, CA private tuitions and many more verticals are booming like mushroom growth.

From above it seems clear that education in the stock market is the new avenue opening fast … and the stock broker firms be it

Angel One, CDSL, Motilal Oswal's, and many more shall also be the main beneficiaries along with their shareholders.

Those with less risk appetite shall be gaining a lot by investing in government companies and shall add to their income in the form of dividends especially with quite a good safety measure. And many shall walk to the bank laughing. Besides there is capital appreciation, which will be there no doubt, for many logical reasons in the coming days and decades to come. So, investors shall be gaining on both ends.

8. Opportunities on Job Front

Job additions are also going to be there in plenty in the coming years as 4 crore self-starters are going to enter the market and even if they employ one person each there would be job opportunities to the tune of 80 million. What to talk of new industries coming and foreign companies investing in India as none of the companies of international repute and worth their name can develop to their potential without having their presence in India one way or the other.

Many more industries coming in infrastructure projects from government side-power generation – semiconductors – even iPhone has started its plant here in India with a joint venture. So, this sector is going to grow exponentially. The number of airports increasing by leaps and bounds, the tourism industry is looking at a great boom as never before. Housing for the poor, all this and many more is going to create jobs for more and more as never before.

9. Investment by Government Companies: Banks

So, mutual fund companies and financial institutions such as life insurance corporations and banks who are in the market are going to invest in the share market in a big way. So, from all angles the in-flow in the share market is going to go many times creating Tsunami in demand resulting into huge opportunity for the investors for the next 20-30 years for sure.

So, this book gains more importance for the investors for making money than ever before.

10. New and naive investors

Even those investors who are naive and do not know the ABC of share market can with little common sense invest in TATA sort of companies – FMCG companies and government companies and can earn handsomely provided they take a long position say for ten years or so. Only thing they need is to keep in mind, select five plus segments and divide the investment equally in these.

They need not go through all this jugglery of reading books, YouTube tips sort of things. Just common sense and lo they shall come out victorious.

"Trees don't grow to the sky, and markets don't fall to the floor."

– Prem Watsa

11. Exports of high-tech innovations and defence goods including planes – fighter jets, armaments – even drones and many more.

This new field has opened up in a great way and has taken a turnaround in an exciting- ways in the interest of the nation besides increasing the morale of the army in a big way.

Not only this will help take back our POK but shall in a larger way help develop this industry in a remarkable manner in the overall interest of the nation, besides creating brand value taking our country in the first three developed countries before long.

The above is simply a small glimpse of the eleven pillars of the Indian economy and there may be many more. However, the above pillars shall give the investors a direction to the sectors which can help them make a killing in industries such as Mazagaon Dock, Cochin shipyard, HAL, Railway stocks, power sector of India, in thermal power, wind power, hydro-electric, solar and others. Not to talk of AI and digital companies, which are going to be the main boosting factors.

As an investor, we should appreciate that knowledge pays handsomely and cannot be stolen at all. Let's use it, apply it, let's falter a little bit here and little bit there. All our failures shall be our assets to save us in the future in any case.

❑

12 Wonders of Stock Market

1. Companies don't benefit directly if they present heartwarming results year after year. It is the investors – shareholders-brokers – lenders and bankers who make money. Workers and white collars working in the company get good salaries and hefty bonuses.

   Indirectly of course their valuation increases and promoters get rich in case they dispose their shareholdings – or the company gets more finance when needs either from the financial institutions or shareholders old or new ones in case they decide to expand or come out with offer of an IPO, Right issues, raise capital or investment through other means.

   Yes, promoters get hefty salaries or packages which of course they deserve.

2. Shareholders or say investors may be earning more than the company in most of the cases as the company itself. By sheer changing hands, the investors can make big money and all combined in due course of time. The gain to investors may outsmart the profit earned by the company itself. A surprise factor.

3. There is no direct addition to the national GDP in the form of production of goods or services. It is all notional.

4. Government earns on all fronts; first tax on the company profits and in addition another tax if the company is paying a dividend. Shareholders paying taxes on dividends. Investors paying income tax on short-term gains or long-term gains.

Even Taxes on sale and purchase of shares too.

5. Mutual fund managers make a large cut and can at times disrupt the market to their will. When institutions buy the share prices rise, and vice versa.
6. There are sharks in the share market jungle where all types of bushes, insects, animals, creatures and all sorts of dangerous species are found ready to pounce upon you to take your life. Share market is not different.
7. The vampires in the share market are there in abundance and are in the form of chameleons difficult for ordinary investors to identify and as such when they make one a victim, one never knows and when awareness comes, it is generally too late.
8. There is no insurance in the share market except your patience, selection and understanding why you have selected a particular share and your real goal, passion and strict discipline, and timely action. The safety mechanism is in your hand, in the form of use of stop loss which is discretionary but hardly used either in normal circumstances or trailing stop losses when the share prices are on the rise.
9. The compounding principle has created many lazy or smart investors - multimillionaires in plenty – them or their heirs.
10. Variety of shares can be akin to species of various kinds found in the cities – villages or far off areas in the dense jungles with their own stamp in nature. This is discussed in the next chapter.
11. Instead of starting your own project, the short-cut route is to target a successful company with a good track record but a sleeping giant—one can acquire a good % of shares in the initial stages and become a director to implement your idea to grow your business.

Whatever you can conceive you can achieve.

If the management is not happy for you to take it over or have his say, one can get out disposing of shares with a hefty amount after successful negotiation.

12. Share market is a paradise for those who know where they are investing, believe in the theory of compounding, have patience, and are consistent. It is hell for those who try to test their luck, are impatient, believe in a quick money-making mindset and above all take it as a Casino.

"Successful investing is anticipating the anticipations of others."

– John Maynard Keynes

❑

15 Golden Rules If You Wish to Burn Your Money in the Stock Market

1. Invest on tips - Invest on rumors - Invest on news.
2. Not planning your investment – if you don't plan your investment – it means you are planning to lose.
3. Not setting your goal- be a boat in the middle of the sea without rudders.
4. Invest in penny stocks – this means you believe in lottery tickets.
5. Not equipping yourself -don't read – know it all approach.
6. Don't care to know why you have chosen a particular stock?
7. You believe in luck.
8. Buy when people are chasing the share on the rise.
9. You interpret the things or situations the way you wish and act accordingly.
10. You believe you are an expert - master of this game of investing – (at times initial small success leads one to think he is an expert).
11. Go on leveraging or averaging the stock – and dig your own grave.
12. Putting all your eggs in one basket.

13. Selling in panic – as all are selling without going through the merits as to why the market is falling?

14. When the pivotal shares fall it burns the mid-caps and penny stocks even more and currently the only thing which counts is the health of the company.

(Nothing else. If the factors are external – need not take any action and if the factors are internal must act according to the situation.)

15. Without realizing that all shares are nothing but heads and tails – timing to buy matters. Same share has made many lose millions and to many it has helped make millions or even billions.

"The secret of financial success is to buy cheap, to sell expensive, to collect the money quickly and pay late."

–Richard Lewin

Risk Free Income – Dividends from Investment

Best way to make use of this wonderful tool available. It is for those who wish to take less risk and still make good money more than the interest rate from bank deposits or government bonds.

These are largely government companies which give very reasonable dividends and have been making investors rich but, in any case the dividends are quite attractive and have been consistent from year to year. There are private players too, such as Infosys- TCS- Vedanta – Hindustan Zinc and many more.

There are more than 250 government companies and one can select 10 companies and start investing for regular monthly income as the companies have been paying dividends on specific months and one can decide or invest in such a manner that he or she gets almost-about equal monthly or quarterly dividends. Also, can add private companies as mentioned above to balance the risk in order to enhance the dividend.

Do some homework and start investing... Homework... shall add to your knowledge as well.

Few shares we are listed here are investors' pets- so you can also, Choose according to your own knowledge.

- Indian Oil Corp: 10.9% dividend yield
- SAIL: 10.6% dividend yield
- REC: 10.2% dividend yield
- NMDC: 9.5% dividend yield
- PTC India: 9.2% dividend yield
- NALCO: 8.3% dividend yield
- Power Finance Corp: 7.9% dividend yield
- ONGC: 7% dividend yield
- Power Grid: 6.5% dividend yield

Besides BPCL, Hindustan Zinc, Vedanta, TCS, Infosys and HUDCO and so on.

And many more railway companies either in finance or infra or steel sector wagons – etc.

❑

Type of Shares – Traits to Identify

Type of Shares

An idea just cropped up that first, all should write down the traits and qualities of the animals, mammals, insects, creatures. After knowing the same, one can then segregate the shares under the same. That would lend credibility to the article in a big way.

a) Python – Anaconda

These shares are in the consolidated zone for quite some time after a great upside swing and behave like a python who after having deer as its food go in hibernation for six months, till the hunger pan rises again.

To my mind Suzlon is behaving like that at the present. Consolidating in the zone of Rs. 35-44. With all the parameters in place can take a jump start if the results in the coming quarters are delivered as expected, the share can zoom in the next two years to around 200 or so. There can be more such examples.

b) Butterfly

Very attractive and you feel like holding the same in your hand and the only thing that comes in your hand is the smell of its wings and nothing else.

These shares are like golden deer in the jungle and lure you to enter the dense jungle to get lost. Examples are HDFC bank –

TATA Elxsi – which reached its higher end and now have fallen by more than 30-40% and waiting for to rise again – good shares no doubt, but for those who bought it at the peak it will take more time and cannot be double than its peak in short run say three years or so. As such one is in dilemma and cannot dare to part with not having the strength to add more which should be the option. However, with most of the investors they end up having zero liquidity, so they are caught in a catch-22 situation.

So, what we get is that you cash-in your cheque before its expiry or validity period.

c) Lion and lioness cubs

These shares may belong to any category but will generally be found in the FMCG category.

Nestle, Gillette, Hindustan Lever although they move slowly but will give huge returns and chances of failure are very remote. They are generally zero debt companies and have potential secured enough as their demand is increasing with time. That is why the lion is called king of the forest.

d) Elephant

These shares are gigantic ones with deep pockets and move in a royal style like those of SBI, ICICI Bank and many more in different categories such as reliance industries, TVS motors and so on.

e) African Elephants

There are companies like **Warren Buffett's – HATHAWAY**, Tesla, Apple, Microsoft under this category and can swallow small companies with so much ease that they go unnoticed.

f) Ass

These shares are like a burden in your portfolio – good ones on account of all the parameters still, no movement and chances shall remain so, costing alternative opportunities and testing your patience giving you hope but after all it is an ass and would be a burden to your portfolio.

Which ones are there in your portfolio? Share them with me for my 2nd volume of this book.

g) Sleeping beauty

These shares are indeed work like Kumbh Karan, or Venus like who enjoy their sleep but still in the minds of most of the shareholders although gigantic in intrinsics value but move damn slowly like that of LIC- State Bank of India from large cap and can find in mid cap and penny stocks as well – when they come out of their slumber, they can make you happy beyond your imagination. Most of them are still there. But we need to develop an art to smell them and add to our portfolio – only out of profits made from some other companies and wait for a miracle to happen.

h) Ant – black

Wonderful species to learn a lot as to team work and in this category comes the shares of Automobile, defence, railway shares, as they come with a baggage of ancillaries such as auto component companies, battery companies, wire companies. Together they can add lots of value and the only thing is, you can decide as to how much of each category of such shares to be part of your portfolio as a percentage of total. As a team for example, Tata motors – where Tata power is working for electric power charging stations, Tata consultancy and Tata technology helping with AI and software related services, Exide batteries or Amara Raja batteries supplying batteries, auto stamping or tata steel supplying steel, forging companies may be identified which are providing forging components.

i) Ant – red

They are and can trouble you if we by chance as an investor selects the group keeping into consideration the same principles as above – say in the food industry the report coming against you – live examples are that of Patanjali products where supreme court issues strict warning for misleading the public through wrong advertisements. The whole chain is affected and with those strictures, the suppliers who were depending upon one client only would suffer and may even come to close down their operations. They bite and give unbearable pain at times. So be aware!

j) Fox

Always luring you to continue in your portfolio – neither they will move in a significant manner up or down but giving you hope every time and years will pass to test your patience. Then hype shall be there and you would add more of that and forget that there are more shares which can give you better returns than this share but we stick to examples like Ashok Leyland, no doubt a good share but opinions may differ.

k) Chameleon

Very dangerous. Like human beings. Change their colour without warning and that happens if we give them a chance. Experience only will save us from this category.

To my mind, shares of this type may be like where there are advertisements to create hype through experts or through YouTube etc. As a wise investor must concentrate on the basic parameters and volume may give wrong indications. Share your input.

l) Dark side of moon – full of new discovery

This category you may find in the penny stocks where one finds this gene as they are laying out of one's views. However, all get their turn one day and one needs to have that knack... for example a news surprised me as to a person taking a broker's license in Switzerland to take benefit of time so that by the time exchanges open somewhere else, one shops for trading in one exchange and selling in another to take difference of price movement before others and make a killing.

m) Mars – A planet

The hot red planet and where most countries want to send their explorers as they expect to find some different metals or materials not existing on earth.

The finding can be time consuming, and may be far away but man's anxiety to know the unknown has been there since the beginning of evolution on this earth planet.

Those who have started taking part now may get a bonanza beyond their imagination one day in the future …maybe 100 years later. Time passes and man's daring shall never fail. There have been examples which are mind blowing and if we take a serious note, we will realise… all is in the mind.

n) Banyan Tree

Just like a mango or apple tree this one encompasses a lot and with time can be a golden hen which shall give you returns for a long time as that has become a huge organisation like Microsoft, Tesla, Berkshire Hathaway of Warren Buffet- Reliance industries. The list can be long enough including Nestle, Gillette, Hindustan Lever, L & T.

In the offing are railway shares – Jio finance and few jewellery companies besides Titan.

o) Sweet-shop

Our portfolio is not only hungry but greedy. Wishes to have all types of shares in it wherever we see there is hope, it will rise and give return without thinking how much? This is human nature.

But with experience like Buffet who says don't have more than 12 shares in your portfolio. Well still we as immatures want to go on adding in our portfolio shares whenever we see any hope in any share.

So, it happens in the early stages of one's career in the investment jungle where there are thousands and thousands of types of plants, some valuable, some not to our mind or because of lack of knowledge, but every plant has some value which is not known to us.

There is a state of confusion and let us understand we cannot enter the various verticals at one point of time say we cannot be a chartered accountant, doctor or an advocate or an engineer at the same time …so we need to choose wisely.

We cannot consume all the variety of sweets available in a sweet shop. Similarly, we need to decide one or few and the same logic we need to follow while creating our portfolio. Well, it is akin to having 100 wives where even to handle one it is difficult. Well jokes apart, we need to confine our portfolio to the minimum and play with few others simply for the sake of excitement to keep our passion and energy on live wire.

The question arises how to do it? Well, it is our individual choice and the purpose of this book is to make you aware of the pitfalls and share the experience of already successful ones and those like me who are still on the learning platform.

To reach a particular destination there are many routes and all may take us to the destination. However, the choice is ours whether we go on foot, on a bus, motorcycle, car, plane or some other mode of transport. So, deciding is more important even if it is wrong. If we are unable to take a decision it is also a decision.

Not taking a decision is also a decision.

p) Dog

Faithful beyond question. There is no other animal which is a friend of human beings than a dog. A friend may deceive, a partner may ditch you, your sibling can ignore you, but your DOG can never, rather would give his life to save you.

This category of shares is worth keeping in your portfolio. Which are these? Can be your own set of shares. This you must choose. It is like which breed of dog you wish to have. For some it can be Tata shares- for some Reliance- for some Government shares and even for some mutual fund investments. All depends upon your risk appetite quotient or your own judgment and experience, and all of you may be right.

q) Peacock

The majestic peacock, with its stunning plumage, is a fitting metaphor for equity shares. Just as the peacock's beauty is matched by its fierce protectiveness when threatened, certain equity shares exhibit similar qualities. When it comes to safeguarding their interests, parent companies can be as fiercely protective as a peacock defending its territory.

Consider the subsidiaries of conglomerates like Tata or Reliance. These shares can be likened to the peacock's precious offspring, shielded from harm by their parent company's formidable presence. Just as the peacock's majestic appearance belies its ferocity when threatened, these shares may offer a relatively safer investment opportunity due to the protective umbrella of their parent companies.

Examples of such shares include Alok Industries, Hathway Cables (under Reliance), Auto Stampings (under Tata Motors), and companies with substantial investments from Tata Investment Co. When evaluating investment potential, it's essential to recognize the protective role of parent companies, just as the peacock's qualities make it a formidable guardian of its domain.

r) Monitor

Where a naughty boy is made a monitor of the class so that not only he is on the right path but controlling the class becomes easy. As the party or a student who could create the disturbance and noise is on the job of handling the same.

Shares under this category are Nestle, Pidilite, Polycab or in other words controlling monopoly sort of entity.

I would even put NTPC and HAL under these categories as a huge investment it requires initially which was not possible for even a large-scale private sector company.

Air India which was privatized by the government has been given back to the Tata's and is now turning around in a big way and instead of being a burden to the Exchequer. It is on its way to becoming a golden egg for the government as it has ordered more than 470* planes for future growth of the country's aviation aspirations and increasing demand with expanding infrastructure in the form of the number of Airports growing by leaps and bounds. The scope is not only immense but shall remain so in the coming decades.

s) Third eye

- Represents intuition, foresight, and the ability to anticipate industry trends and disruptions.
- Just as the third eye in mythology grants insight and perception, investors need to develop this ability to foresee changes in the market.
- This involves staying agile, informed, and aware of emerging trends, technologies, and innovations.
- Demergers, mergers, and acquisitions can unlock hidden potential, and investors with a "third eye" can capitalize on these opportunities.
- The phrase "No risk, no gain" and "No pain, no gain" emphasizes the importance of taking calculated risks and being proactive in investing.

Similar situations uncovered opportunities when Palestine's Hamas attacked Israel and in support of Israel India and America

* Indian Airlines' Recent Orders:

- Air India: 470 planes (250 from Airbus, 220 from Boeing) [1]

- Akasa Air: 150 Boeing 737 MAX planes [2 3]

- IndiGo: 500 narrow-body planes from Airbus [1]

came forward to provide all types of assistance and thus on the opposite some other countries like Russia and China started offering help to HAMAS supported people.

That offered opportunities to companies in abundance. We need to see here which companies could gain and in advance buying shares of such companies. Here we are not talking about who is right or who is wrong and what our ethics are or should be!

However, as an entrepreneur I would not support HAMAS under any circumstances and would not deal with them against Israel. Just like Tata's when they were offered lucrative deals by Pakistan they refused straight away.

t) Frog:

- Symbolizes hidden opportunities and companies that may not be immediately visible but can emerge during specific market conditions or seasons.
- Just as frogs become active during rainy seasons, certain shares may become attractive during particular market cycles or trends.
- Investors need to identify these hidden gems, which requires knowledge, experience, and a deep understanding of market dynamics.
- The ability to spot these opportunities is both a science (analysing data and trends) and an art (applying intuition and expertise).
- The examples you provided, such as war, natural disasters, and global events, illustrate how entrepreneurs and investors can capitalize on emerging opportunities by being aware of market shifts and adapting quickly.

Investors need to develop their "third eye" to anticipate market changes and identify hidden opportunities, much like the frog that emerges during rainy seasons.

u) Rat

The rat, often underestimated, possesses remarkable qualities that investors can learn from. Its ability to navigate complex environments, adapt to new situations, and prioritize survival is a valuable lesson for investors.

The story of the rat cutting the net to save the lion illustrates its resourcefulness and sharp instincts. Similarly, investors can benefit from being cautious and prepared.

The quote "Go to the Mouse, You Foolish Investor, and Learn" highlights the importance of diversification. A mouse never relies on a single hole for safety, instead, it creates multiple escape routes. Investors should adopt this strategy by spreading their investments across different asset classes, sectors, or shares.

This approach helps mitigate risk and ensures that a single investment doesn't dictate the entire portfolio's performance. By "bifurcating" investments into at least five different segments, investors can minimize potential losses and maximize returns.

The rat's ability to reach grains in a go-down and finish them efficiently demonstrates its focus on survival. Investors should similarly focus on preserving their capital while aiming for growth.

Let's summarise the key takeaways from the rat metaphor:

1. **Diversification is key:** Spread investments across different assets to minimise risk.
2. **Be prepared:** Anticipate market changes and adapt your investment strategy accordingly.
3. **Prioritize survival:** Focus on preserving capital while aiming for growth.
4. **Stay resourceful:** Continuously learn and improve your investment approach.

v) Monkey

The monkey's habit of copying others can be a valuable lesson for investors. While it's natural to seek guidance from experts and successful investors like Sanjeev Bhasin, Mukul Aggarwal, or Rekha Jhunjhunwala, blindly following their investment decisions can lead to trouble.

Just as a monkey mimics actions without understanding the context, investors who follow others without doing their own research may find themselves in a difficult situation. They may struggle to exit their investments or fail to generate profits, simply because they didn't comprehend the underlying reasons for the investment.

The phrase "Suno Sabki, Karo Man Ki" (listen to everyone, but do what your heart says) emphasizes the importance of using your own judgment and research when making investment decisions. It's crucial to understand the company's "horoscope" – its financials, management, industry trends, and competitive landscape – before investing.

Key takeaways from the monkey metaphor:

1. **Avoid blind imitation:** Don't follow others' investment decisions without understanding their rationale.
2. **Do your own research:** Conduct thorough research and analysis before making investment decisions.
3. **Use your own judgment:** Trust your own instincts and don't rely solely on others' advice.
4. **Understand the company's fundamentals:** Study the company's financials, management, and industry trends before investing.

w) Snake – poisonous one and non-poisonous ones

The snake metaphor illustrates the destructive power of fear and panic in the stock market. Just as most snakes are harmless, but the fear of them can be deadly, investors' fear of market downturns can lead to poor decision-making and significant losses.

The story of the thief who died from fear of a snake bite, despite the snake being harmless, highlights the devastating impact of fear on investors. When the market declines, many investors panic and sell their shares, often resulting in heavy losses and a long-term departure from the market.

However, if investors had the knowledge and experience to understand that the market tends to rise over time, they could overcome their fear and capitalize on opportunities during downturns. The key is to differentiate between poisonous (high-risk) and non-poisonous (stable) investments, just as one would distinguish between venomous and harmless snakes.

In 2008, I had gone through the same factor although I was not afraid, my mistake was, I played in greed on borrowed money as has been shared why I wrote the book?

Practical knowledge or learnt knowledge can help us overcome fear and can help those whose risk appetite is higher to take it as an opportunity to add on every fall, especially those shares which are solid from all parameters point of view

Practical knowledge and a well-informed approach can help investors:

1. **Overcome fear and panic:** Develop a level head and make informed decisions, rather than emotional ones.

2. **Identify solid investments:** Focus on shares with strong fundamentals, just as you would recognize harmless snakes.

3. **Take calculated risks:** View market downturns as opportunities to add to your portfolio, if your risk appetite allows.

4. **Avoid greed and leverage:** Learn from your mistakes, like playing with borrowed money, and adopt a more cautious approach.

x) Aurat – Women- or an Angel

The Aurat metaphor, represents the intricate and nuanced nature of certain investments, much like understanding a woman's complex emotions and behavior. Just as it's challenging to fully comprehend a woman's mood, character, and vibes, investors must carefully analyse and navigate delicate investments to avoid missteps.

The comparison to a woman's attractive smile and charm highlights the allure of certain shares, like those in the IT sector (e.g., Tata Technology, Asian Paints, Tata Elxsi). These investments may seem appealing, but their volatility and unpredictability can lead to mistakes, such as selling too early or missing out on potential gains.

The metaphor warns against making impulsive decisions based on short-term market fluctuations, just as one should avoid making hasty judgments about a woman's character. Instead, investors should adopt a patient and informed approach, recognizing that these shares may be subdued but have potential for long-term growth, much like Titan.

Key takeaways from the Aurat metaphor:

1. **Approach with caution and nuance:** Delicate investments require careful analysis and consideration.

2. **Avoid impulsive decisions:** Don't make hasty judgments based on short-term market movements.

3. **Patiently accumulate potential winners:** Identify and invest in shares with long-term growth potential, even if they seem subdued.

4. **Understand the complexity:** Recognize that certain investments, like women, are complex and multifaceted, requiring empathy and understanding.

y) Mirror

The mirror will tell us what we look like – we will look the way we are and so must accept the truth.

In case of doubt about your inner fight – discuss with yourself in the mirror with your copy as if he is another person and most probably you may find the right answer. Mirror is our reflection and if we think on a serious note, we will find we like to hear what we wish, and thus get biased. So have a direct dialogue as if you are your enemy and how the other person is looking at you.

So, love yourself as you are and you are the best. Have confidence in yourself and never doubt your wisdom and underscore yourself on any point. Remember, the value you put on yourself is the value people will put on you. And remind this aspect to the person in the mirror.

z) Rose

Gives and spreads essence so wonderful be it of rose or sandal or any other flower!

The real value of the rose is on a higher pedestal, but if we see below the same, there are thorns which can hurt. So, every share is like a rose after selecting the same through test from its parameters. Do remember when to enter and when to get out? All depends upon your goal, as a trader, as an investor or as a wealth creator.

These remind us that hurdles shall be there in any case in the form of thorns but warn us as to be aware of them to let them hurt you.

The rose metaphor beautifully captures the dual nature of investments, much like the flower's essence and thorns. Just as a rose spreads its wonderful fragrance, a well-selected share can bring significant growth and value to a portfolio. However, beneath the surface, thorns can cause harm if not handled carefully.

This metaphor reminds us that:

1. **Opportunities come with challenges:** Every investment has its potential risks and obstacles, like thorns on a rose stem.

2. **Selection is crucial:** Choose shares that meet your parameters and goals, just as you would carefully select a rose.

3. **Timing is everything:** Know when to enter and exit, depending on your investment strategy (trader, investor, or wealth creator).

4. **Awareness is key:** Be mindful of potential hurdles and take steps to mitigate them, just as you would handle thorns when handling a rose.

The rose metaphor encourages investors to be aware of the potential risks and challenges associated with each investment opportunity, while also recognizing the potential for growth and value.

aa) Eagle

Can see from as far as 5-6 kilometers and can smell and see its prey and decides to catch it with a precise plan and measures the distance and succeeds to pin-point the location correctly measuring its flight path and pouncing with precision attacking and catching its prey with surprise.

This quality as an investor we need to develop and see the future, like an eagle. A surprise angle is as important as in the war too, the same principle applies.

The other thing we can learn from an eagle is when it reaches a particular age, gets old and when its beak loses its sharpness and becomes useless, it starts breaking it knocking it against the stone and bears pain which is unbearable. After this, it gets new wings and a new beak and can fly again with confidence to start the next journey afresh.

That is what as an investor we need to learn that after losing only we get another life and the loss is not a loss but an investment.

The eagle metaphor embodies the qualities of a visionary investor, capable of:

1. **Long-term vision:** Seeing opportunities from afar (5-6 kilometers), symbolizing the ability to foresee market trends and potential.
2. **Strategic planning:** Measuring distance, flight path, and precision, representing the importance of thorough research, analysis, and planning in investment decisions.
3. **Surprise and adaptability:** Catching prey with surprise, illustrating the need to stay adaptable and responsive to changing market conditions.

4. **Renewal and resilience:** The eagle's ability to break and regenerate its beak, symbolizing the capacity to learn from losses, adapt, and emerge stronger, with a renewed perspective.

   As investors, we can learn from the eagle's qualities:

1. **Develop a long-term perspective:** Look beyond short-term gains and focus on sustainable growth.
2. **Plan strategically:** Conduct thorough research, analyse market trends, and make informed decisions.
3. **Stay adaptable:** Be prepared to pivot and adjust your investment strategy as market conditions change.
4. **Embrace renewal and resilience:** View losses as opportunities for growth, and be willing to re-evaluate and adjust your approach.

The eagle metaphor inspires investors to soar to new heights, with a clear vision, strategic planning, and the resilience to navigate challenges and emerge stronger.

bb) Reflection

We are our own reflection as we have discussed in the mirror heading. What we feel about others is nothing but our own reflection.

When we see so and so is a cheat – actually if we think seriously, we see the mirror image of our own character to a large extent. Believe it or not - it is a fact and truth as I have learned. Though I do not like hearing it.

Hard to accept it may be, but largely it is the only truth and fact.

The reflection metaphor highlights the concept that our opinions and perceptions of others are often a reflection of ourselves. When we judge or criticize others, we may be unconsciously revealing aspects of our own character, values, or biases.

This metaphor suggests:

1. **Self-awareness:** Recognize that your perceptions of others may be a mirror image of your own thoughts, feelings, and experiences.
2. **Projection:** Be aware that you may be attributing your own qualities, motivations, or flaws to others.
3. **Introspection:** Take time to reflect on your own character, values, and biases to better understand yourself and your perceptions of others.
4. **Empathy and compassion:** Practice understanding and kindness towards others, acknowledging that their actions and behaviors may be a reflection of their own struggles and experiences.

In the context of investing, this metaphor can be applied by:

1. **Recognizing biases:** Acknowledge how your own biases and experiences may influence your investment decisions.
2. **Self-reflection:** Regularly examine your own thought processes and emotions to make more informed, objective investment choices.
3. **Empathizing with market sentiment:** Consider the emotions and experiences of other market participants to better understand market trends and sentiment.

By embracing the reflection metaphor, investors can cultivate a deeper understanding of themselves and others, leading to more informed decision-making and a more compassionate approach to investing.

cc) Crow – she-crow – Koyal

The voice of the crow is so sweet that one stands still to hear it and starts enjoying the same.

It is a gift of God. When we get lost and are immobilized by its sheer sweet voice, we get astray and miss the bus. For these attractions can cost us like alluring of some shares, we let the time pass and lose a big opportunity. Need to be focused on our main motto that we are here in the share market to make money and not to lose the opportunity and not to lose the money. And for that, focus is what is required.

The crow metaphor represents the allure of distractions and the importance of focus in investing. Just as the sweet voice of the crow can captivate and immobilize, attractive but potentially risky investments can divert attention from the main goal of making money.

This metaphor cautions investors to:

1. **Stay focused:** Prioritize your investment objectives and avoid getting sidetracked by enticing but potentially costly opportunities.
2. **Maintain discipline:** Stick to your investment strategy and avoid impulsive decisions based on emotions or short-term allurements.
3. **Avoid distractions:** Be aware of the potential for distractions, such as market volatility or trendy investments, and stay committed to your long-term goals.

4. **Keep perspective:** Remember that investing is about making money, not getting caught up in the excitement or novelty of certain investments.

By embracing the crow metaphor, investors can cultivate the discipline and focus needed to navigate the share market effectively and achieve their financial goals.

dd) Palm tree

The tree metaphor represents the journey to success in the share market, where the fruit of success is often out of reach and requires effort to attain. Climbing the tree symbolizes the need for:

1. **Experience and skill:** Developing the art of climbing, representing the acquisition of knowledge and experience in investing.
2. **Perseverance and hard work:** Recognizing that easy gains are often of little value, and that true success requires sweat and effort.
3. **Strategy and planning:** Using stairs, technology, or other tools to climb safely and efficiently, representing the importance of a well-thought-out investment strategy.
4. **Resilience and adaptability:** Embracing the variety of challenges and opportunities in the market, just as trees adapt to different seasons and environments.

The comparison to various insects, animals, plants, and natural phenomena highlights the diversity of investment strategies and the importance of learning from nature's examples.

The mention of volatile shares with qualities like volcanoes, storms, or black holes serves as a reminder to:

1. **Be cautious:** Approach potentially risky investments with care and thorough research.

2. **Diversify:** Spread investments to minimize exposure to any one volatile share or sector.

3. **Stay informed:** Continuously update knowledge and adapt to changing market conditions.

Nature indeed offers valuable lessons for investors, emphasizing the importance of persistence, strategy, and adaptability in achieving success in the share market.

I urge all investors to grade the shares from your point of view under any of the above categories and why?

After I wrote the metaphors I took to AI and asked for guidance and surprise awaited me.

For, the AI tool refined the same logically and in proper sequence which not only amused me rather put me in awe.

Let it be a game and enjoy playing it. That way you can learn and add to your experience a lot.

No matter how much we analyse, one thing is clear and that is: no knowledge can predict the exact outcome but direction only. But even if we are moving in the right direction, it is preferable to know the direction rather than not- knowing the direction. Slow we may move but the principle of compounding shall definitely put us in the company of wealthy people or in a billionaire club.

❑

Some Tit Bits

1. Luck factor

What is luck? People say I have been unlucky in property or share market or in a job or what not?

Opportunities are there for everyone but depends upon all of us to wait for the same or create for us?

It is in our hands largely. But to quell any doubt, I was given to understand in my early career by my seniors that the luck factor is there but very rare.

For example, two friends had a two-acres of field each side by side alongside the river. Both worked equally and laboured equally, feeding properly and taking care of the paddy in equal measure. Both the fields were ready and it was harvesting season in the coming week. But lo what happened? Flood occurred and one friend's field got destroyed completely whereas both were almost equal and would have given equal results in terms of grain sale. But one lost everything and to the other nothing happened. This is called luck- when you don't have things in your hand. External factors no one can control.

Another example which a banker friend of mine narrated to me against my version "that I do not believe in luck."

He said lift your one leg. So, I lifted my right leg automatically. Now he asked me to lift another leg, without disturbing the first one. Can we? No. he said that is what luck is. Once you have chosen an alternative, how can you opt for another one at the same time?

For example: you decided to be a CA and thus invested 4-5 years in this. You could decide to be a doctor or advocate or whatever it may be – once you have decided there and then you have opted for your career. Even kings think of doing something but they have chosen and that is their fate. That is their luck. That is their destiny.

All of us have our role to play in this universe. Enjoy the same with happiness and let's remember "Rich people may not necessarily be happy, but happy people are more likely to be rich."

2. Rich and Poor

Who is rich and who is poor?

All of us would say he is rich and that he has millions of rupees. And B is poor because he has no money and hardly makes his ends meet.

Another friend of mine would say we have limited demands and by sheer greedy nature. The MORE we get, the more we want. And thus, go beyond our resources and thus remain much less happy as compared to the one who maintains himself within his budget.

A banker friend of mine told me the secret and I liked it.

You are rich if your income is Rs 100 and you spend Rs 99.

And you are poor if your income is Rs 100 but you spend Rs 101.

I really got it! But to act upon free advice one hardly gives importance.

Opinions can differ… my friend who is a great management consultant- and NLP teacher. Said in one of our BNI meetings **"All is in The Mind"** How true!

3. Know It All

There are people less educated – don't like reading books nor listen to the motivating audios or go through any spiritual classes but know it all attitude never leaves them.

What I have learned is that education or degree is not that important as having common sense and anxiety to learn more and more.

Knowing it all attitude is one such negative trait that is going to cost heavy one day. Little knowledge is a dangerous thing. Neem hakeem khatra Jaan.

There is no use arguing with them. Khalli ghara bajje ghana – empty vessel makes more noise.

A real knowledgeable person believes in "MORE We know, we know, Less, we know"

4. One Step at a Time

Success is never accidental. Behind it there is sweat-labor-discipline -focus-belief that "I can do it," I do not know and still need to practice. Sachin Tendulkar was practicing at night. Bolt, who won the 100-meter Olympic race and broke the record in less than 10 seconds had practiced for the last 25 years day in and day out. No one can imagine that the iceberg which we see in the sea, is just 10% above sea level or what we see, and 90% is under the sea.

The real thing is to initiate the first step and go on taking a step- have patience and the moment domino effect takes place the engine shall pick up from diesel engine to petrol- to electric and won't take time to become a rocket.

"A thousand-mile journey starts with just one little step."

Your first step is what counts. Once you start your journey people shall come forward to assist you- God will send its force without your knowledge. Law of attraction shall start working silently.

Only one condition: you must have full faith in your vision – and that means you are just a step away from success!

5. Generating good income-creating wealth or creating true wealth

By trading alone, one cannot create wealth, yes abundance of income may be earned, but as far as becoming wealthy is out of question.

Wealth can be created only in the long term because the law of compounding starts working and that is a miracle in itself. For that one needs to have patience. Patience is also a struggle and most of us shall quit the ground before real fruit is ready to be plucked. Because most of us are impatient to wait till it is ready.

Above that is the concept of true wealth. After creation of wealth, one needs to be on the ground and must understand that material things have limited value.

True wealth lies in one's satisfaction and that satisfaction quotient can come from different sources. From pursuing philanthropy, to creating a great and best hospital, creating an educational institute, or helping young women to create employment opportunities and whatever it may be the crux is to create value in someone's life who deserves but does not have an opportunity.

6. Never Cry over the Spilt Milk

I remember I was in 3rd standard in Arya Samaj School, Lodhi Road, New Delhi-110003 in the year 1953. Our teacher Mr Ahuja asked the monitor to bring a glass of milk from the canteen, our school used to be in tents with no flooring of any type.

When a glass of milk came, he kept it on the table and intentionally put it on the floor and asked the students to put it back.

How could it be? So, he said in life never cry over the spilt milk. The point had gone to our head. That is the reason I still remember it and quote it here.

This lesson has helped me a lot in my life.

7. Good to great

The book Good to Great emphasizes the importance of continuous improvement in achieving success. Whether in our careers, businesses, or social endeavors, we must aim to be better than our best. The secret to success lies in making a little extra effort, which can make a significant difference.

Consider the Olympics, where a gold medallist is celebrated, while a silver medallist is often forgotten. The difference between the two is often a fraction of a second. This tiny margin highlights the importance of that extra effort.

Successful individuals like Sachin Tendulkar, Virender Sehwag, and Virat Kohli demonstrate the value of hard work and dedication. They have all put in the extra effort required to achieve greatness.

Now, it's your turn. Remember, the difference between good and great is often just a little extra effort. Will you strive for greatness?

8. Domino effect

I learned about the domino effect from Akshar Yadav, a marketing expert. A fascinating example illustrates this concept:

A temple, 100 kilometers away, attracted pilgrims who would offer apples to the abundant monkeys. Initially, the monkeys would pick up the apples, but the tourists' sweaty hands would leave sand on the fruit, making them inedible. Over time, a few innovative monkeys started washing the apples in the nearby river and enjoying them. As others observed this, they began to follow suit. Within 30-40 days, all the monkeys had adopted this new behavior, demonstrating the domino effect.

This phenomenon applies to our investment strategies as well. Consistency and persistence are crucial, as we never know when our efforts will reach a tipping point, triggering a domino effect in our portfolio. Sustainability, faith, and perseverance are essential for achieving success.

9. Change

As the saying goes, "Change is the only constant." Continents shift, rivers alter their course, and human destiny is shaped by habits, persistence, and passion. Our upbringing, social circle, reading, and thoughts influence our development. Even in the midst of challenges, change is inevitable. A slight direction change, hope, and consistent effort can lead to a desired outcome.

Remember, the domino effect can take time, but it will happen. Faith and determination are crucial. Prayer can provide support during difficult times. Our belief in the outcome plays a significant role.

A great quote summarizes this: "If we keep doing what we're doing, we'll get the same results." "To bring change, we must change our approach." This emphasizes the importance of adapting and trying new methods to achieve our goals.

10. View

We all perceive the world differently, just like our unique tastes and thought processes. This diversity is the essence of life and innovation. It's essential to respect others' views, as they're shaped by their environment, biases, and experiences.

In politics, individuals may prioritize personal interests over the nation's, hoping to change their fate. However, others may see through this and view them as foolish. Ultimately, the public has the wisdom to discern.

Similarly, in share trading, various forces are at play, and ordinary investors can be taken advantage of. To succeed, we need to develop new filtration techniques through experience and learning. This will enable us to navigate the market effectively and make informed decisions.

11. Life span

Everything in nature has a lifespan. Be it planets, companies, human beings, animals, insects, mammals, vanaspati, or whatever we see.

Similarly, we even have a lifespan for our good times. Or life span for our problems too. Time is a great healing factor. And with time we get accustomed to riding over our problems. However, we need to be aware of it and should have faith to turn things in our Favor. That is possible if we have developed our habits accordingly and have faith in the GOD in our own way.

The knowledge that there have been people who lost everything and still not surrendered to fate. They know that they can create opportunities and as such not only that, they survived but have achieved the impossible.

So, we too can change and overcome any problem be it in the share market or in our life.

Hope sustains life. In 2008, when I lost Rs 70 lakhs in one week I surrendered and left the market for good. Had I been lucky to have a mentor the fate would have been different. But as mentioned above, never cry over the spilt milk, I did forget that and braved my way – that was luck. Good or bad I don't know.

But that incident was not a loss, rather today I see it as an asset and that is the reason this book, is before you.

12. Drink Water by Digging Your Own Well

The stock market often appears as a mirage—tempting yet elusive. However, it becomes simple if we focus on understanding businesses rather than obsessing over shares or stock prices. Successful investing is built on personal judgment, thorough research, independent decision-making and the acceptance of personal risk. Following others blindly without drawing your own conclusions or trusting your instincts will not lead to success.

The stock market rewards what I call the 3 P's: **Performance, Patience and Perseverance**. Let's delve into the stock market through the wisdom of great thinkers, expressed through their quotes. A powerful quote can distill profound insights into a single sentence.

For instance, the quote,

"People who wonder if the glass is half empty or half full miss the point. The glass is refillable."

— Unknown

This reminds us to view situations with optimism. There are always alternatives, and adaptability is the key.

"Progress is impossible without change, and those who cannot change their minds, cannot change anything."

— George Bernard Shaw.

This quote emphasizes that in the stock market, being rigid won't lead to success. Flexibility, the willingness to shift your views, and adapting to market conditions are essential if you want to generate profits.

Warren Buffett captures a timeless truth: *"The stock market is a device for transferring money from the impatient to the patient."*

This is where Einstein's theory of compounding becomes invaluable. The power of compounding works wonders in the stock market—but only with time, which requires patience.

Peter Lynch similarly warns: *"You get recessions, you have stock market declines. If you don't understand that's going to happen, then you're not ready, you won't do well in the markets."*

This reminds us that ups and downs are natural in the stock market. Those who endure setbacks and learn from them are the ones who eventually succeed.

Angela Duckworth adds another layer: *"Enthusiasm is common. Endurance is rare."* Success in the stock market is not about temporary excitement or bursts of enthusiasm. It's about sustained persistence, consistency, and focus. Motivation is like daily maintenance—you need to keep fueling it with purpose to stay the course.

> *"If you have built castles in the air, your work need not be lost; that is where they should be. Now put the foundations under them."*
>
> **— Henry David Thoreau**

This quote is a call to action. Dreaming big is important, but even more crucial is laying the groundwork for those dreams. In the stock market, it's never too late to start building that foundation.

Phillip Fisher highlights a vital distinction: *"The stock market is filled with individuals who know the price of everything, but the value of nothing."*

Investing is not just about chasing high prices or trends; it's about value hunting—finding opportunities when others overlook them. Identifying the "gold in the dust" is an art that can lead to long-term success.

Finally, Sir John Templeton's caution rings true: *"The four most dangerous words in investing are: 'this time it's different.'"*

Market conditions change, but the fundamental principles of investing remain. The difference between those who make money and those who don't often comes down to understanding this.

The stock market may appear as a mirage, but armed with patience, persistence and the wisdom of great minds, one can navigate it successfully.

❑

8 Super Secrets Unlocked to Succeed in Any Business

Once you enter any profession – business or industry that would generally fall in between the following either one of the categories or mixed one.

All occupations or businesses can give you enough money – within it lies the gold, depending largely upon how we look at it.

People have made billions from garbage even. So, no business is bad. We need to have the third eye to see the potential and ways and means to discover the potential in it. Then not only dream but act. Application is the key.

Secrets are:

1. **It is capital intensive**

    a. Like nuclear power station for generating electricity

    b. Oil refinery -like that of Reliance

    c. Reusable Rockets - Elon Musk

    d. Mass production

However, one needs to keep abreast with the latest technology, change in technology like cars from petrol and diesel to electric-solar – ethanol and so on.

2. **It is based on some formulae, secret or patented etc. and is of daily consumable-nature. Either the main product is**

needed or consumables are required or refills needed time and again.

You are either addicted to taste- or quality and use.

KFC, Gillette Products, Coca-Cola and so on

3. **Game of Numbers**

Necessity or addiction or daily need such as:

Tata Sky, Jio Mobile, Gas Companies, Ola, WhatsApp

4. **Technology Driven**

iPhone, Microsoft-Windows, Aircrafts, Drones, Air driven cars and so on.

Utility of drones cannot be under-estimated; they have multiple uses – as a watchdog. For creating 360 angle photographs- for farmers used for spraying- for military use- for carrying parcels, food and what not.

5. **New technology – innovation or ideas**

   a. Edible plates and spoons

   b. Roads by waste of plastics or from other by-products

   c. Electric cars, buses

   d. New economically produced solar products – or solar energy

   e. New technology in farming either in the air or muddy waters or like

   f. AI or digital payment software etc.

6. **Out of the box idea and implementation of the same economically**

The need is production of the same product economically and producing distribution channels keeping all points in view to market it by creating demand for the same or adding value to some existing product substantially. Mobile was not required but by creating value and demand it has become an extended part of our body.

The same thing is happening in the gaming industry where more than any value the younger generation is becoming addicted to it and helping the gaming industry. Minting money like soft drinks which are harmful to the society but still selling like hot cakes.

You should be the first company to bring it to the market.

You are the first to get it patented.

You are the first one to get copyright registered.

First one to start a franchise of the same.

7. **Brand value**

Creating brand value, like Colgate, iPhone, Air India, Samsung, Sony, Microsoft and so on.

8. **Artificial-intelligence – Digital technology**

Now drones are being developed at a mass scale for very many diverse uses. Even for distributing food, parcels, for creating artificial rains and defence. These are gaining irresistible importance.

Now to do well in business we need to come up with some unique way to have either one of the above or a mix of one or more according to the demography, utilization, use or effectiveness of the strategy.

Must keep in view the changing technology and chances of getting the current machinery or technology obsolete. Change of taste, hitting the product in the proper district or state or a country. Gold ornaments—designs of north cannot succeed in south or taste of north India may not last long in south.

Our once-cutting-edge rotary telephones have become obsolete relics. In the future, even today's smartwatches may be outdated as new technologies emerge. We might see communication devices integrated into our skin or projected through smart glasses. Technology is advancing so rapidly that companies like LG have already developed transparent TV screens for everyday use.

The game of numbers is one thing and selection of any products of daily use not necessarily in food items, we need to think and pursue.

With the increase in population the scope is immense and change in technology makes it even more challenging, however the secret lies in turning the idea into action -plan and persisting with it.

Besides looking at the above, one has to follow systems or create them to make the business run on auto mode – or even in the absence of human interference one way or the other.

The system is one thing which gives grease to the business and in the current scenario is a must. The other ingredient which is required is to know why? As Simon sneak points in his book, "Start with why?"

If we start with why? How will find its answer automatically.

The above shall in many ways help us regarding any company in which we are investing, some good insight as to why we must invest?

For example – the game of numbers shall help us deduct that as we know the number of demat holders is going to double in the next five years from about 150 million to 300 million, the demand for shares is going to rise slowly but definitely and the total market which is worth 4 trillion now is going to cross 10 trillion. The reasons are many. For instance, per month SIP collections are increasing by leaps and bounds – and going to be not less than 50000 crores by 2030 may be and that would be infused in the market thus prices of shares would automatically be on the fire and on the rise.

Many government projects in heavy vehicles – aero-space industry as well as railways infrastructure are on the rise and all this shall result in substantial increase in employment and thus more demand for shares. The basics is in the coming years keeping pace with the development the share index is going to touch 100000 in any case.

Point to be made here is that no article in this book is irrelevant and all have in them the secret hidden to decide based on your realizing the positive inputs.

Now the time has come where real nectar is waiting for you in part 2 of this book.

It is essential to go through the first part which sets the stage for the reader to absorb simple secrets revealed to you in your journey to be a Billionaire.

My heartfelt thanks to you for sparing time for your own benefit to learn how to achieve financial abundance. In true sense chasing your passion …your dream… on your own terms!

End of PART 1 of the book. It is not a full stop. It is the beginning of the new journey where the real secret lies.

❑

PART-II

No More a Secret for You– How to make Millions from the Stock Market?

It is an open secret now.

Since you know the secret NOW, how to make millions from the stock market? Let's go to the next class and there lies the secret to multiply those millions to at least a billion.

Do you doubt it? So, keep your doubt with you till you will say Oh! Yes, it is possible and can be done.

By now you are convinced that it is not difficult at all to make millions, especially under the present environment when most sectors are growing full throttle or all sectors are going to go full throttle in the coming days and years. Especially under the present Government who have a vision of inclusive growth.

Your next part of the journey which is still under wraps is going to be revealed.

By now you must realize you have been promoted to the advanced course and unless and until you have gone through the first part of the book, chances are, you will miss the boat to be a billionaire. Yes, I as an author can say it with my experience, that it is so.

To achieve a billionaire status is very easy, once you understand the share market and the valuation part of your business which can multiply manifold by acting upon this section written for your benefit only.

Yes, there are certain conditions and few of these are:

1. You are a manufacturer in auto-FMCG- chemicals and many more verticals of industries.
2. You are in the service industry.
3. You are in the hospitality industry.
4. You are in the pharmaceutical industry as a trader or/ and as well as a manufacturer too all the better.
5. You are in the IT sector with a unique solution and have certain clients or you have a product that can help save millions in the banking industry or processing industry or hospitality or AI innovation etc.
6. You are not an employee or a shopkeeper without ambition.

There can be many more verticals and that can be discussed on merits and feasibility criteria.

❑

Preface

The logic behind dividing the book in two parts has been a quirk of fate for the benefit of the reader who wishes to be multimillionaire many times over.

An idea struck that most of us are unaware as to the valuation of our business and how to encash it / or capitalise it for the shareholders and equally for the management.

Real hard and smart work can work wonders in enhancing our wealth many times over if we follow with discipline and work-smartly to bring IPO within reasonable time which can vary from strength of the management from one sector to another and discipline which need to be followed to achieve the same in a meaningful-manner.

The same has been explained in this 2nd part of the book in a simple manner.

Enjoy the same and cherish the journey to be a multimillionaire in a reasonable time frame.

❑

Success Journey of Few Companies

To make this comprehensible for the reader, our next step is to select out of out of 10 readers and Champion friends, who have agreed to undertake this journey with the author and let us see how many of us reach this journey to its logical end?

That will show strict discipline- setting our goal- having a mentor and like Arjun all of us see the eye of our target and nothing else.

And this starts with our first board meeting, the agenda of which is set and copy of the same is shared with the readers herein below:

First Meeting of the Board of directors of champions Click N Connect limited is hereby called on 15th of May 2024 at its registered office at 11 A.M to discuss the following:

Present

Avinash Nispaksh	Champions Click N Connect P LTD
Pushpender Singh	Ambient Technology (AI and solution)
Supreet Singh	PSYCHO-CARE Pharma
Ankit Wadhwa	Fun bytes
Abhishek Jain	Digital and AI platform

Ranjit Singh	To Farc - office furniture
Narender Singh	Classic 44 - Bakers and new venture Bharat Bakers
Tejinder Singh Mokha	Certified financial planner
Dr Jitender Singla	Multi-specialty hospital
Gaurav Mehrotra	ISO certification

1. Agenda: To bring out the IPO of all our companies for at least 200 crores of rupees by 2029.

   To hold our own equity of at least 51% of the whole.

   To vet the business plan from now onwards from some big consultancy company which has to be selected after due diligence and experience whose advice and experience in the field of bringing an IPO's is confirmed and are of integrity.

   With a target of zero debt company or negligible debt as compared to assets.

2. All the directors shall present their projected turnover for the next five years and target by 2028 year-wise and what hurdles they expect in this journey.

   How to overcome the same with the cooperation of one and all?

3. Only those who are optimistic about this plan shall be opted as directors of the company which has its own plan to bring out the IPO and in which we all are partners or stakeholders.

4. It is not compulsory to be a shareholder except for a minimum of Rs 1 lakh and that too be paid in four equal installments with option of buying up to 5% of the equity within one year or such equity as may be decided on individual basis

for mutual benefit. Those who can otherwise support can also be taken in the board provided their support is genuine and valuable. This shall be discussed in detail in the format as per white paper prepared.

5. Avinash narrated that he has selected the board of his own as he sees a lot of potential in all of them and is interested to support in whatever manner to achieve the target of each one of them without any obligation.
6. Main objective is that, it is possible to be a billionaire in 5 to 8 years starting now. Billionaire means one is worth 100 crores at least as per valuation of his equity stake as per market capitalization.
7. We all agree to hold one meeting every month and sub committees shall be formed and any idea if put forward shall be discussed without bias and in mutual benefit. Action shall be initiated accordingly to achieve our main objective.
8. All of us should at the outset put a self-imposed discipline and act in a positive manner so that it can be achieved and shall prepare the goal affirmation.
9. All expressed their affirmation that they have full faith in the idea and are ready to proceed with zest and passion. ***As no one is going to lose in any case, all also affirmed that all of us take this as a challenge and as a sport.*** But all of us should succeed.
10. Any other matter with the permission of the chair.

As there was nothing else to discuss further, the meeting adjourned with a vote of thanks to the chair.

In the board we can have one advocate- one financial expert, one chartered accountant. Whom to induct shall be done with the consent of all the directors.

They will be guest advisors and once the company takes off – can be appointed advisors with a mutually agreed fee as may be discussed in mutual benefit.

Largely friends from the champion chapter of BNI have been roped in with potential to be billionaires out of many.

Summary

The very first thing out of the above was that all directors present their next five years projections by the next board meeting to be held on 15th of June 2024, duly vetted by their chartered accountant.

Also, it was suggested that all shall assist each other seriously.

Now the steps to be taken are almost clear and have to pursue them with dedication and within a time frame.

Audit has to be done of all the participants to see that under the framework of what they are doing at present, is it conducive to bring about the IPO in the coming years? If not then in that case the white-paper is to be prepared concerning that company after discussion with them and correct the course of action. The purpose being to fall in line to achieve our main objective and that is to launch an IPO of all companies one after the other.

❑

Funbytes

Second Meeting of the Board of Directors of champions Click N Connect Limited is hereby called on 15th of June 2024 at its registered office at 11 A.M to discuss the following.

Minutes of the last meeting held on the 15th day of May were read, approved and signed.

Mr. Ankit Wadhwa representing his company Funbytes, presented his budget and projections for the next five years. He showed consistent growth in turnover from 2024 to 2028. To fund his expansion plans, he proposed a loan of 12 crores to set up a factory and install new machinery. He planned to repay the loan by selling 20% equity to franchisees.

Ankit aimed to increase the number of franchises from 60 to 530 by 2027. He introduced a new concept where franchisees could open two more outlets with the help of expert management and bank approvals. This would increase their income to at least a million rupees per month.

The company also introduced local Flavors in their outlets, which were successful. They planned to open bigger outlets in places like Ayodhya and Varanasi, serving only vegetarian items.

Ankit's expansion plans were ambitious, with a target of 1000 outlets by 2028. He had already hired an experienced team of experts to help with location selection.

One director joked that Ankit's plans were too big, but Ankit replied that he was confident in his ability to achieve his goals, just like how Jio Mobile had disrupted the market.

The directors agreed to support Ankit's plans and suggested forming a team to select the right candidates for the job. They also decided to invest in the business as sleeping partners, with a minimum guarantee and profits based on turnover.

Heads for all departments were appointed to have a central control system and duties were allocated to improve efficiency. All this resulted in smooth operations and marketing and sales heads were quite experienced to promote the products through various channels to create brand value.

All this helped him move towards his goal of bringing IPO sooner than later.

❑

Ambient Technology

Now all decided to discuss the case of Pushpender Singh Manchanda ji of ambient technology.

His projected statements were shared with everyone in attendance, all went through broadly and there it was found that it had to be redone as had been prepared by a novice non-technical person but the whole picture seemed to be very bright and promising.

A. Sports segment

1. His company's expertise on developing software in sports can take the company a long way. How to impart technique to newcomers in the sports segment he chooses, what are the main points which one needs to keep in mind and training module – tricks- salient points and practical examples – the rigorous schedule – how to maintain and diet sort of things every question which comes to the mind of the seeker is there in the software and available at the touch of the button.

2. The games can be chosen as there are many and initially can be taken from the Olympics schedule.

   Various technical teams to be formed with a sole agenda to develop the software containing all feasible angles, rules, criteria for selection, training schedule and diet considering the weight and physical attributes. MASS- and from which state one belongs as every corner of India has different weather and different food habits and taste. Innovation being the main theme.

3. Weather conditions also to be taken into consideration.
4. A rigorous schedule is the need of the hour. Military type.
5. Self-created tools on the software can be developed for the benefit of those aspiring for a career in sports.

B. Automobile segment

Power sector – thermal – wind- solar- hydro- and many more and various ways by improving technology- time saving devices- efficiency incremental technology

C. To decide on segment where there are few or none of the companies working

D. One can choose a particular segment or two and work consistently on that to create value.

Expertise on one segment can create brand value but it does not mean that the company is not capable of delivering on other segments. Depends largely on the opportunities offered. Once when one is in the market, let's say when we talk of Barista – which means coffee but do they serve coffee only? No, there are so many other items developed according to local taste.

So, it was decided to go through the same and put it in proper perspective for the purpose of presenting to the shareholders and some hiring of experts from TCS, Wipro or Infosys may be contacted who have shown exemplary work in their organizations.

There are very many small companies in the market which are developing fast enough as the market is so big and companies too many, who are doing wonderfully well and are in the lookout for various solutions for their businesses either in private sector or Government sector.

There are many public sector undertakings around 250 plus, which are going to develop as big mammoth companies in the coming future.

How to locate them and present the solutions which Ambient has developed or are capable of developing to grow in revenue 1000 times what we are doing at present.

Also to form collaborations with small developing companies or take over management control of those companies which can gel with our objectives properly.

We need to work out the various departments who may be working on different verticals be it manufacturing- zero inventory- payment security methods, AI in banking sector- hospitality- and travel sector.

The other one thing which one of the directors suggested to Mr. Pushpender that like TCS- Infosys is we should hire recent graduates having requisite technical knowledge as trainees in thousands of numbers as the business is developing from America and Europe which will result in recruiting them at later stage besides saving lot in expenses on account of hiring charges.

When the number of young employees start working as trainees- companies shall be billing their clients on hourly basis with much less payment is another big saving thus increasing profitability for the company. This was a secret for TCS and many big up-coming companies. It used to serve a double purpose. One the new young team was being groomed in the best environment and the talented ones selected according to his or her trait and secondly the chances of getting the diamonds became easy.

Regular flow of money in the company is very important and for that one has to develop some software without which one cannot survive. There are virtually many fields on which the company can start working for the clients and also learning from the market such as companies like Busy Bee, Tally accounting software, sales force etc. where the revenue is generated year after year in progressive manner thus enriching the company's cash coffers automatically.

This type of software can be developed in many sectors which they once used to maintain it in any case and update the same with new features added. Case in point is that of Microsoft with many more companies like Reddington dealing with AutoCAD and many more thus resulting in continuous inflow of money.

Target for the next five years was redrafted with the help of experts within this group and it was found that in the next five years the staff shall increase from 58 to 300, and 1000 in the second year, 4000 by fourth year and 10000 by fifth year end. Increase in profitability rising from 3 million US $ to 700 million in the fifth year. Earning profit to the tune of 20% and above of the revenue.

There were many hurdles which were discussed, mainly the tough competition in the field. It was settled that when we have some new features developed the company making use of the same shall be willing to pay. No one pays for nothing except when he is gaining from using this software, therefore once we know the new feature which we are providing, no one else can at least for now, there is no reason that they would not buy. In this instance our marketing team must play an active role.

Secondly one has to develop the system of lease rent also so that the burden to the party is not immediate.

Many other small points were discussed and it was decided to address them as the time shall pass. As there is no such problem where a solution cannot be found out. Necessity is the mother of all invention.

No doubt, some vital points like rigorous training and diet plans could be further emphasised and inserted into the software for auto-guidance. Here are some suggestions:

- ❖ Rigorous training schedules with specific exercises, sets, reps, and rest periods
- ❖ Personalised diet plans based on athletes' goals, body type, and nutritional needs

- ❖ Automated reminders and alerts for training and nutrition plans
- ❖ Progress tracking and analytics to monitor athletes' performance
- ❖ AI-powered coaching for real-time guidance and feedback
- ❖ Integration with wearable devices and health trackers for seamless data collection
- ❖ Customisable training programs for different sports and athletes' levels
- ❖ Injury prevention and rehabilitation protocols
- ❖ Mental preparation and mindfulness exercises

Incorporating these features into the software can provide a more comprehensive solution for athletes and coaches, setting Ambient Technology apart from competitors.

So, it was decided to go on discussing the same every month in the committee formed for the purpose.

❑

Bharat Bakers

Owner Shri Narinder Singh

Experience 40 years in the bakery business.

It was decided to take up the case of Shri Narinder ji Owner and partner Classic 44 Bakery, for next meeting and in the meantime, he shall be discussing the same on a regular basis so that all of us should fall in line as per our goal for all of us to achieve billionaire status. And the case of Dr. Jitendra Singla for starting a chain of hospitals.

Shri Narinder Singh ji of Classic Bakery 44, placed before the committee his company's projections for the next six years.

He narrated the first history of the company which he along with his elder brother started.

The hard work they had put up in cooperation with each other resulted in 7 shops in different parts of the city and all are doing reasonably well contributing to the coffers of the company.

Lately it has come to the notice of the management that there exists excellent scope not only in tri-city but in the whole of Punjab and nearby states. The logistics have to be taken into account and improved and hiring of experienced staff along with new and fresh candidates to look after in a professional manner.

It was pointed out by one of his advisors that the name should be changed for few of the new stores and slowly and the three different names to be promoted side by side.

One under the present management, continuing the same number of items and improving in display and brand management. The second one to be promoted keeping in consideration for dividing the company for family reasons and keeping the love among the two families a balance of power on- mutually agreed principles.

Here one needs to understand that Classic 44 bakers must identify with one item which should be famous and that should carry the name.

And people should know the classic bakery by that item. It can be cake-rusk, pastry or a Chinese or French baked recipe. Say cheesecake, chicken pot pie, veg pot pie or for that matter any item people get a mouth-watering feeling by the name itself.

To promote the same one should do marketing such as one plus one for a month or so or till Diwali or the coming festivals.

Innovative schemes have to be launched on various occasions such as Bhai-Dooj, Diwali, Holi and so on and the preparation has to begin six months before. A special R & D team must develop all the festival's schemes in advance. Not only six months back rather for the next few years has to be ready in advance and changes incorporated from time to time as the experience grows.

It is the smallest things which matters and whenever a new idea comes, it must be added in a notebook and timely incorporated in a new scheme. Overall, the goal is to add on revenue and thus profit and fatten the bottom line for the shareholders.

By now the number of outlets had increased from 7 to 22 in the second year and 47 to third year, crossing 100 by the fourth year of owned outlets. And the number of franchisees starting from third year were slow to add but they also increased from 3 to 42 by the end of fourth year. In these 15 were such where we had a token partnership of 26% with the condition, they could buy back the same from us any time 3rd year to 5th year time. Or after that on an agreed amount in mutual benefit.

The profit grew considerably and in the initial stages the sale was little slow in certain stores, or outlets but through backing of the marketing team efforts the same was increased to a comfortable level.

An increasing number of outlet companies started adding on to the iced vehicles from 3 to 12 and they used to move to desired stores in the morning from 4 am to deliver the products throughout tri-city and nearby states.

Not only that, to help the aspiring students on their threshold careers, a special scheme was also launched to furbish the trucks and make them CHALTI-FIRTI bakeries and all the legal requirements were being provided including finance from the banks and public institutions. These were doing better and besides being innovative because of screen display helped improve the publicity of Bharat Bakers in a unique way.

This concept took time but soon became a household name and provided breads, cakes, biscuits, pastries and a few delicious items ready to eat and fulfilling. Special drinks were a quick favorite of students.

The past four years profitability was as under

(figures in crores)

	2024-25	2026	2027	2028
Share capital	1.5	2.00	3.00	4.00
Sales	37.56	123.20	280.46	512.76
Franchisees fee + royalty	00.11	1.56	3.42	7.78
Share of profit from partners	.00	.70	1.67	3.23
Total A	**37.67**	**125.46**	**285.57**	**523.77**
Cost of machinery	2.20	5.40	7.50	10.30
Cost of sales	15.30	49.87	112.60	216.00
Administrative exp.	12.80	39.30	90.01	155.20
Depreciation	.33	.81	1.12	1.54
Total B	**28.43**	**89.98**	**203.73**	**382.74**
GROSS PROFIT A-B =	**9.24**	**35.48**	**81.84**	**141.03**
Interest	1.00	5.00	0.00	00.0
Management fee	1.90	6.25	14.00	26.00
Taxes	1.20	4.80	24.00	48.00
Net profit	**5.14**	**24.23**	**43.84**	**65.03**

There are very many cumbersome details such as taxes, management salaries etc. but this has been done to give a general idea as these are imaginary figures to make the reader understand the basic principles. And these are sales growth, profit growth consistently.

(*NOTE: it is pertinent to note that no single trait or ratio or zero debt concept will work in all the cases. That could be disastrous thinking. The PE may be thousand and still the chances of growth of the company may be still young and huge potential may be awaiting and vice versa.*

Company may be doing much better and more promotion is being done through television channels and it may flop.

There may be a company doing well and progressing fast and one change in Government policy may render it unfit as an investment target. So, the basic thing is, use of common sense, computing various aspects and coming to sane judgment as has been described in 31 parameters in part one of the book. Even those are simply an indication and not the final verdict.)

The progress was the result of day and night working on different ideas and experimenting on the same in quick succession. Though in the initial stages the profit grew as the number of outlets increased from insignificant to considerable amount but in a haphazard manner. However, the consistency will be there, now onwards as the company has reached a reasonable scale from where it is time to consolidate till the next step is taken.

Now the company is ready for launching the IPO and the valuation of the company was way above normal and keeping future possibility the premium was decided way below the market could absorb. Thus, helping share-holders procure a bonanza.

The management could foresee the billionaire journey at its sweet beginning.

Another alternative was placed before the board and that also sounded fine from all angles.

It is in partnership with the elder brother and time has come when because of the next generation entering, it is best to segregate the business amicably for the peace of the next generation. So, keeping that in mind the following is decided.

A new company is created as a dummy with the understanding of coming out with an IPO and providing different platters by creating brand value besides that of Classic bakers. However, the new entity has to be done as a consultant but in actual it belongs to Narinder ji and family. But the same is kept under wraps for the purpose of smooth separation with the existing family.

So, Bharat Bakers or such new name is considered and domain name registered in the name of that dummy company for the time being in such a manner that no one can know that it belongs to Narinder ji.

The whole project was developed in the light of this new policy which although he appreciated but was afraid too, knowingly it was the right step in the interest of one and all. Because looking into the future and taking or grasping the opportunity is essential.

So, after due consideration it was decided to go ahead. And he is an advisor to the company on a token fee as a consultant. Because ultimately the company belongs to him only as per a secret agreement entered in the presence of an advocate of integrity from the BNI group.

A new factory land was purchased after considering various pros and cons in a Lal Dora village and a loan was applied for the same as the project cost came down to Rs 50 Cr. Where the bread unit, biscuit unit and namkeen unit was being built separately with most modern packaging units also being in house. Even the latest technology for printing and packaging was incorporated.

The big kitchen was also planned with a rooftop restaurant as a brand development started with a big bang manner attracting the attention of who is who in the hospitality industry.

All looked so good but it had its own limitations and one day it was decided to go it openly and prepare a plan to open at least many outlets with a plan on the board for the next decade.

A company was hired to give projections and cash flow and profitability keeping into consideration various segments and profitability of each segment. As per plan few experts were hired from Haldiram, Dabur, ITC and an agreement was entered into with 50 or so sweet shop keepers who had created a name for themselves and few of them to be bought at a later stage. The strategy was formed with an eye on the 20 years as a development plan.

An idea was to open at least 5 outlets in the first year and 20 the second and 50 the third to 150 by the end of five years.

Two brands were developed, one known as Bharat Bakers and another few under the different names such as Kasam, Dadi Ma, Chai ji and accordingly in the south with a different name so as to help to identify the local merge of identity.

The original name was used to develop in own stores and the other brands for distribution to all those who were not franchisees but wanted the product under their own names, it was essential to do so on account of taking benefit of large-scale production. And cutting down on cost per kg.

The best profitability started paying off on namkeens and that was economical too. Research and development section was developed to keep innovation of new products being developed and tried.

It was found that there is vast scope in this line and the number of items can be in many thousands, but it is slowly being realized to concentrate on 300 items and specialize in them.

Many different models were created to facilitate different categories and timing and quality being of paramount importance, besides maintaining delivery schedule. Finance department being most crucial it was specially agreed that all sales must be on cash basis, and in case of regular customers of wholesale, advance cheque to be taken against delivery within 15 days or credit like that of Hindustan Lever.

The progress was the essence for developing the business keeping into consideration local tastes and blending the same with different cultures thus experimenting the same successfully. The same proved a wonderful idea and was liked by couples who were both working.

To Create a successful bakery business using technology to streamline operations, improve efficiency, and enhance customer experience. Advice sought from the AI further helped produced the following:

Key Features: All the below

1. **Automated Recipe Management:** Store and manage recipes digitally, with options to scale ingredients, convert units, and generate nutrition labels.
2. **Inventory Management:** Track ingredients, supplies, and products in real-time, with automated alerts for low stock levels and expiration dates.
3. **Production Scheduling:** Create and manage production schedules, including batch processing, to optimize labour and resources.

4. **Quality Control:** Implement quality control measures, such as temperature and humidity monitoring, to ensure consistent product quality.
5. **Customer Management:** Manage customer orders, preferences, and loyalty programs, with options for online ordering and delivery integration.
6. **Supply Chain Management:** Connect with suppliers for automated ordering, tracking, and payment processing.
7. **Data Analytics:** Track sales, profits, and customer behaviour, with data visualization tools to inform business decisions.
8. **E-commerce Integration:** Sell products online, with options for delivery, on-site pickup, or in-store pickup.
9. **Digital Marketing:** Utilize social media, email marketing, and loyalty programs to engage customers and promote products.
10. **Staff Management:** Manage staff schedules, training, and performance, with options for time tracking and payroll integration.

Technical Points:

1. **Cloud-based Software:** Utilize cloud-based software for scalability, flexibility, and remote access.
2. **Integration with Hardware:** Integrate with hardware devices, such as ovens, mixers, and scales, for automated data collection.
3. **Mobile App:** Develop a mobile app for customers to order, pay, and manage loyalty programs.

4. **API Integration:** Integrate with third-party APIs for payment processing, delivery services, and social media platforms.
5. **Cybersecurity:** Implement robust cybersecurity measures to protect customer data and prevent hacking.

By incorporating these features and technical points, the bakery business can streamline operations, improve efficiency, and enhance customer experience, setting it up for success in the competitive bakery market.

Here's an added marketing strategy to outsmart the competition:

Marketing Strategy:

1. **Unique Selling Proposition (USP):** Develop a USP that differentiates the bakery from competitors, such as "Artisanal Bakery with AI-Powered Customization" or "Bakery with a Social Cause."
2. **Influencer Partnerships:** Collaborate with social media influencers, bloggers, and local celebrities to promote the bakery and create buzz around new products.
3. **Content Marketing:** Create engaging content (blog posts, videos, social media posts) showcasing the bakery's story, recipes, and expertise to attract and retain customers.
4. **Email Marketing:** Build an email list and send regular newsletters with exclusive offers, new product releases, and event invitations to loyal customers.
5. **Loyalty Program:** Implement a loyalty program that rewards customers for repeat purchases, referrals, and online reviews.

6. **Strategic Partnerships:** Partner with complementary businesses (coffee shops, restaurants, event planners) to offer bundled services, joint promotions, and expanded reach.
7. **Experiential Marketing:** Host events, workshops, and classes (e.g., baking classes, cake decorating, pastry making) to create memorable experiences and build brand loyalty.
8. **Referral Marketing:** Encourage customers to refer friends and family in exchange for rewards, discounts, or free products.
9. **Online Presence:** Optimize the website for SEO, ensure seamless online ordering and payment, and maintain an active presence on social media platforms.
10. **Data-Driven Marketing:** Use data analytics to track customer behaviour, preferences, and purchasing habits, and tailor marketing efforts accordingly.

Outsmarting the Competition:

1. **AI-Powered Marketing:** Utilize AI tools to personalize marketing messages, predict customer behaviour, and automate marketing tasks.
2. **Secret Menu:** Create a secret menu or exclusive offers for loyal customers or influencers to generate buzz and encourage word-of-mouth marketing.
3. **Gamification:** Develop a gamified loyalty program or promotional campaign that rewards customers for completing specific tasks or achieving milestones.
4. **Surprise and Delight:** Surprise customers with random acts of kindness, free products, or exclusive offers to build brand loyalty and encourage positive reviews.

By incorporating these marketing strategies, the bakery can outsmart the competition, attract and retain customers, and establish a strong brand presence in the market.

Remember, a well-planned strategy, combined with innovative thinking and effective execution, can help businesses like Ambient Technology and the bakery outsmart the competition and achieve their goals.

In one of the board meetings of the company we had the opportunity to discuss the case of TRI-City Multi-specialty hospital of Dr. Jitender Singla. His dream project

❑

Tri-city Multi-Specialty-Hospital

Dr. Jitendra Singla

His background was very inspiring as his journey to be an orthopedic doctor specialising in knee ailments had gained popularity in his field and a name to the hospital as well in his community.

He had a dream for many years to have a hospital where treatment according to the income of the person be charged and none who could hardly afford had to go without proper treatment.

Had a soft corner and thus he wanted to create a hospital with the highest standard and hygienically best not only in India but abroad too.

He met the chief minister through a doctor friend and got allotted 20 acres of land in the heart of tri-city at Rs 1 per sq. meter with a condition that at least 25% of the facilities shall be for the poor people of Punjab and their treatment has to be done absolutely free. That is what he wanted and as such the seed was sown and now the major task was to be handled and time be spared from hectic day routine to realize his dream.

While preparing the project report with the help of his CA friend he got goosebumps and got the surprise of his life when figures started rolling before him.

With a 300-bed hospital he was thinking that the total cost shall be around 150 crores but to his astonishment the projected statement which was before him came to the tune of 450 crores. And time taken being 30 months from the date of all approvals in place.

Total area under construction came to be around 6.5 lakh sq. ft except parking space. It was estimated that parking space for a 300-bed room hospital shall be minimum for 1000 cars as covered space and around open space for 1000 cars was needed.

X-ray rooms, lab rooms, doctor's-cabin, nurses' cabin and mess for the DRs as well as for nurses and administrative staff. Marketing staff, canteens for public as well as for workers, receptionists, waiting rooms and general area for 100 lifts and children play area. In house laundry area, computers, printers, dresses, area for medical shops, eye-wear and maintenance of lifts. Plumber, electricians for air-conditioning, staff hiring and retention problems. He was thinking he had taken on a huge task and started doubting whether he would be able to cope up with the task in hand and would he be able to do justice with the same.

Nothing is easy and he thought that there are many hospitals running all around and how would they be managing? So why cannot he? That idea infused in him positiveness and he started to think positive and remembered the quote that if one starts thinking of problems only, they will manifest and he will spend his life in that world where solution is miles away. And frustration and negatives shall crop up wholesale and thus ruin the project.

So, he needs to think positive and solutions shall crop up as we move on. As such he started preparing a deadline for every aspect such as hiring an architect of repute who has already built few hospitals.

He started off having services of some civil contractor and decided that he shall have that contractor who is already in construction for many years and has few projects running around the tri-city.

He discussed with his CA to prepare the project report in consultation with some experienced CA who already has helped some running hospitals and has been associated with the company from the beginning. Also to get him some expert banker who could manage financial closures and all aspects as to expected needs and time schedule.

He also started approaching his doctor friends who could take a space in the hospital and contribute besides renting a space for long term but invest in equity or deposit for 7 years at the very reasonable interest.

For hiring the best doctors, nurses and administrative staff and every type of staff to arrange for their interviews and finalizing the same preliminarily so that at the right time they could be hired and their training starts well before the hospital starts finishing.

He felt light and there was an issue as to buy the necessary furniture- tenders for central AC and lot many other machineries, like X-RAY, hundreds of such for various tests, have to be bought and there were various companies so he started sending them mails and started comparing which machine is better and why and what is the cost and what is the difference if any. All the tasks were delegated with proper control and at last his passion now was at its height. Passion is infectious and spreads like a plague in a good sense and thus all gelled as a team, working to finish their tasks to see the hospital opens sooner than later.

The hospital building was coming up fast enough as all were given deadlines without compromising quality. Discipline being the main parameter and was understood by one and all from bottom to top hierarchy working overtime to see the dream hospital opens sooner than later.

Another plot of two acres within the compound on the corner was developed for housing of doctors on one side and housing for nursing staff on the other corner with 200 units in total. To help the patients, continued service of expert doctors as because of pressure of time working day and night it was a necessity rather than a convenience.

One other aspect was the security staff which was so huge it could not be comprehended that around 150 such staff shall have to be appointed on 8 hours shift – there being three such shifts.

Regular monitoring of the activities was essential and cameras were placed on all the buildings inside as well as outside and this was a huge burden on the financial front.

Cost of various software was another cost unknown at the time of contemplating the hospital. Number of bathrooms for ladies and gents on all floors separately for public and attached bathrooms for nursing staff and doctors were another requirement which had a great impact on the cost of construction of the hospital.

Even garbage dumps were created and latest technology was utilized to make use of that to use as fertilizer for plants on the vast space and greenery created to make the ambience five star.

Solar panels were used to generate electricity as an additional security measure and save on the cost of running and continuous flow of electricity was taken care of. However, a separate grid was provided by the government for hospitals as a priority.

Similarly, peons, helping staff, gardeners and so many other miniscule items were there which had to be taken care of.

Rainwater harvesting and water sprinkler systems in the garden, along with advanced water reuse technologies, have been implemented to conserve water.

After surmounting so many issues it was decided to start one part of the hospital wing and within three years the full hospital and all its wings started working.

It was a huge task to bring the hospital to survive the initial period and slowly the breakeven was achieved after three years and now the rush was so great that it seemed that the facilities-provided still fell short of requirements which were growing faster than expected.

The other black spot was analysed which was insurance companies where the game was different and needed great caution. Merit cases were being rejected and non-merit cases were being passed on account of graft spreading and needed a sane and sensible solution.

Though late but by 2028 it was realized that the IPO can be launched only after 2030 and not before. For the hospital to come to reasonable profit could be achieved only by then and to bring it before would be catastrophic.

Well after so many hurdles and lot of experience Dr. Singla with ample of experience gained was now almost ready for the next big step where he could feel proud of his, dream project to go in for branches, first in metros and then in tier two cities and villages on a different- models which could serve the humanity.

Purpose is now clear and the secret is open before you as to how to increase your wealth by dint of your hard and smart labour and capitalising the same at an opportune time. Haste and impatience will spoil the race to be a billionaire.

It is the process which has to be followed with discipline, with an eye for a successful launch of an IPO and for that as discussed above one has to consistently fight the odds to grow consistently with integrity and discipline which shall be the foundation stone besides the acumen of a hardcore businessman. In brief, that is care of the customer, vendors and people involved with the company in any manner. All have to be looked into. All have to be taken care of. The vision of the company should be such that each person is not only aware of it but should gel with its heart and soul.

The welfare of the working force from all angles such as housing, education of their children, training of the whole work force be it labour or management trainees must be taken into account which shall result in greater efficiency and thus save huge amounts in terms of maintaining discipline. This obviously shall result in more production and more profit for the company and its shareholders.

All the 10 board of directors who were in different verticals started their journey with lots of enthusiasm and vowed to continue with complete dedication following the above principles. Their participation in the board meeting and help which all of us received from each other supported on all fronts thus making efforts in one direction and that was to bring the IPO in the next 5-8 years.

It was clear that those who believed in consistency and discipline were ahead and those who took it leisurely were lagging behind. All though all of us were supporting each other with heart and soul with one motive that none of us should fall behind and must succeed in equal measure.

There was a tough healthy competition among us in terms of winning and who shall be the first one to bring his company's IPO keeping into consideration the basic principles in mind and not falter at all. As one mistake could ruin or spoil the whole exercise. Keeping each one on one's toes and just like a navigation tool adjusting the same to reach the destination following the locked target.

All knew that even a small support can lead to success and never misjudge any advice, as at times we ignore solid advice resulting in an accident and thus failure. Any overlooked mistake could cost not only time but lots of money too.

All the ten participants had selected one other person as their accountable partner to be accountable to each other for his accomplishment that helped a lot in moving forward with a pace desired to be successful.

With time passing, three directors fell behind and seven were sure to reach their destination. They were trying to the best of their ability showing exemplary discipline. For they knew and have understood that this is the only way to achieve their goal of abundance and richness.

The best part was all the stakeholders were aware that it is not the money which is important but they loved the challenge, for they knew real happiness lies in the welfare and satisfaction rather in accumulating wealth. Once we work sincerely to the best of our ability, money shall follow automatically. All were not chasing money but their dreams. Money was the by-product. They also knew that to make money they must delegate and make use of their time in planning and execution. This thinking changed the whole scenario.

Champions Click n Connect also succeeded in their mission to launch the IPO successfully. Creating a valuation of around 8 billion with 60% holding the main promoter Mr Avinash Nispaksh donated 95% of his holding as you could see in the prologue of this book.

How he achieved this shall be discussed in the next chapter in brief and what the aspiring readers need to take out from that is left to their best of judgment and understanding.

The journey if explained shall take thousands of pages, but here only the nectar shall be served. For, by now, the reader has reached a level of great understanding as a graduate in share market complexity.

Frankly speaking, as I embark on this writing journey, I'm simultaneously discovering numerous ideas and gaining profound insights. One concept leads to another, and along the way, hidden lessons and unexpected epiphanies emerge, revealing themselves effortlessly. This journey is full of delightful surprises.

Basically, everything is so simple that we make it complex by overthinking.

Following were the guidelines on which we worked and started our journey in Champions Click n Connect Ltd.

1. The goal was to launch an IPO by the end of 2028.
2. Projections were made after discussion with all the departments starting with sales, marketing, finance, production, research and development, and HR.
3. Training modules were decided in advance to bring all the stakeholders to know the company's vision and see that all gel into it.

4. Common agenda and motto being decided so that all were in unison to achieve and put their efforts into it wholeheartedly.
5. Discipline was assigned priority along with ethics, morality and care of the customer as top of the agenda.
6. Sales targets were decided by the sales team heads with their regional and international heads for the next 5 years taking into consideration expected upheavals or competition or new technology being adopted on a large scale.
7. Designing team was assigned to see how cut in cost of production can be achieved and with consultation with R & D department assignment to replace items with alternatives, without compromising on quality and at the reduced cost to be one step ahead of competitors.
8. Production department was aligned to see that the required production shall be there according to orders as expected on zero inventory basis and capacity or extended capacity if at all required can be arranged within a short notice period.
9. To keep the margins if not on the higher side but maintaining them to pre-existing levels is a must. For, that novel methods for improved packaging and premium products to be launched with novel schemes was given priority.
10. Proper incentive schemes for vendors, suppliers and workforce were also taken up to motivate on auto-mode.
11. Exports to different countries were given due importance and opening of branch offices in different parts of the country and internationally was given due importance it deserved. Through partnership mode to control expenses and bring in win-win situations for partners too.

12. Keeping pace with the latest technology was prioritized and implementation was the key in all sectors of the company.
13. Reasonable dividend to be distributed was to be given top priority if we need to bring an IPO successfully without harming the financial resources of the company.
14. As a special provision, the Chief financial officer was given the responsibility to make arrangements for financial resources via various financial instruments on long term basis at the minimal cost. With an option to convert in shares at a particular discounted value within a three years period.
15. Availing funds from financial institutions, either through loans or equity shares, can be beneficial for the company's financial health.
16. Regular follow up of the data and corrective measures to be taken immediately as and when needed and well in time without going through the usual authority chain which was made simple and fast. The power was given ab-initio.
17. So, the overall solution of every expected problem or line of action to be taken was pre-decided as far as possible. Even in case of any untoward incident happening, responsibility according to the nature of the problem was to be handled by the respective heads without going through the usual chain of approvals. He had complete authority to decide on the spot. Just informing the MD as a mere formality.

All the departments were motivated to achieve the company's objectives and thus was one of the top agenda of the company.

Avinash Nispaksh, gave his presentation which in brief covered a unique way to develop the business of trading activity on selected items through this novel concept based on '8 super secrets unlocked to succeed in any business' which has been mentioned in the last part of the book.

It was pointed out by the MD of Champions Click n connect Ltd. that the main profitability comes from buying cheap and selling at the high price. In this direction he narrated a story of the power of numbers.

That comes from the number game – power of numbers. This lesson was understood by the MD from a saint in one of the sessions, he had attended a long time back in Mumbai.

Where the saint informed that there was an association of Jain's community consisting of around 5000 business men. Almost 100 or so wanted to buy luxury cars such as Audi or Mercedes or BMW and when they approached seeking quotes for the same for 100 + cars they were surprised to recall, almost 30% discount was offered and they availed the same. It shows the power of numbers. Similar is the case of suppliers to D-Mart and stores like Jio and the like to have the best rates much lower than the market and thus survive in the competitive world.

Similarly, one can if one has numbers the suppliers can be roped in to give a very high discount with the result to create win-win situation for both the parties.

His overall plan was to have three lakh members across to this platform and slowly that to become a centre of activity for all the members to have contacts with any member of the group for their promotion of the business.

The revenue model was prepared and the whole scheme was put up for implementation cautiously for any one mis-step could ruin the whole game. Different chapters were allocated to the regional levels and had centre command.

Many issues cropped up and the main hurdle was to have the software for the whole operation and keeping track of all the activities and data based on AI so that certain reminders were set on the go in such a manner that the follow-up was done automatically to bring in more business and delivery done through AI. Not only that, even the credit in terms of points or commission was to be released to the respective party after due diligence through checks and balances so that no mistake happens and no payment is made without being due. And all participants get their part of the promised share or commission in an auto mode.

After achieving the initial number of members to 10000 it was decided to go full throttle and introduce new membership schemes like ordinary – silver, gold, platinum and titanium etc.

The best part was membership, although it goes higher and higher but to the member it will cost nothing as they would be given goods worth more than the cost of membership fee.

For instance, if the person becomes a silver member by paying a fee of say Rs 1100 he shall be given goods worth Rs 1300-1400 so that he feels duly satisfied.

Similarly, when a person becomes a platinum member for Rs 3100 he shall be given goods worth Rs 3500-3900 or so.

Besides that, he shall be given certain privileges to contact the members of the company directly.

As the number of members increases the members who wish to promote their product can be charged a certain sum to promote their business and thus increase the company's profitability.

Every month two products shall be introduced for the members at an unbelievable price and thus making use of numbers game and bargaining power that members get quality products at a nice discount and the company gets its profits not less than 10% of the MRP.

In time, the same can be increased to one product every week and increase the promotional activities so as to reach membership to 3 lakhs at least within the first three years.

How to increase the number of numbers? Why should one register? These questions must be answered first and planning has to be done accordingly.

Slowly the members can be given the opportunity to invest in housing projects – farm lands and cottages in hills where the cream of profit lies. Similarly, loans for consumer items and such other new fields without going into any risk except as a source of creating a market for the members and sponsors alike.

So, the main hurdle lies in developing the marketing strategy to increase the number of members at a fast pace.

How to go about it? Keeping into consideration the vast development in the economy of the country and fast development all across the country in all sectors be it defense, FMCG, chemical sector, infrastructure, and moreover government policy as to inclusive growth is going to be the backbone of the economy in the coming decade.

Because of inclusive growth the likelihood of the economy taking a quantum jump should not be a surprise.

The increase of the number of members to 3 lakh or more in a span of three years is not a daunting task if planned properly and acted upon systematically by creating a model for the benefit of members.

Here we need to create many alternatives and one of them can be to give one book free to download worth Rs 350. And all those filling up the google form and giving correct answers to a few questions shall be eligible for a prize of Rs 10000 every quarter.

The other incentive could be a pair of wrist watches or even a mobile worth 20000 at half the price.

But the question arises as to how to get in touch with millions of people to have 3 lakh members to enroll.

So, in this direction following ideas were put forward by the research team and are being enumerated herein under:

1. There are 150 million demat holders. So how to contact them?
2. There are billions of shareholders of various companies – select a particular company, say the first 10 top companies and offer them membership.
3. There are billions of mobile customers – can we offer them somehow to reach them and do the needful?
4. How to reach and have contacts with the youth who are in colleges – throughout India and abroad even and prepare some admission form which can guide as to their purchasing power, standard of living and such as their mindset so as to help in offering them what they prefer and like.
5. There can be many such alternatives which need to be explored to reach the modest target of three lakh members to set a stage for take-off to make the company successful financially and in the service of shareholders as well as to members.
6. Various marketing strategies to be innovated to draw attention of various segments be it corporates, government white

collars or from military segments in active service or retired population.

7. Various schemes for elderly population taking into consideration their needs, aspirations- etc. have to be launched but how to reach them is a task which needs an out of the box idea to convert them as members.

8. All existing members to be rewarded to add a few of their friends as members can also be exploited with proper incentives as well as obligation sort of.

Not only that it should be a career for few of the aspirants, therefore the need to make it rewarding enough.

All said and done, the next stage shall bring in opportunities way beyond our expectations. One cannot even think in its wildest of dreams. Such as mutual fund investments, share brokerage firms, franchisees of few top brands or develop our own brands side by side to not only add to profits but generate employment opportunities to women and young aspirants.

One thing can lead to another and the only thing is how to manage the same quickly and fund these with minimum capital.

Only thing from the above which is clear is that a company needs a well-defined software to handle and use of AI is natural. For without it the chances of going astray shall be very high and following the same to its logical end may be difficult indeed.

So, this way the company started its operations and created various heads keeping in view their capability and how they can earn handsomely to make the company huge in terms of its reach and brand value.

Research & development wing besides logistics were the main pillars on which hanged the overall development of business. Guiding principle being JIO launching where just in 73 days 100 million subscribers were added creating a world record.

That sort of execution is required to make the company in the service of members and knowing that it is care which matters. Care of customers, members, suppliers or vendors, staff of all categories and looking after the smallest of things with miniscule details to take care of.

Similarly, in the beginning itself it is generally clear who would lead the pack and succeed in bringing out its IPO first and show path to others.

The best part was whatever little contribution one could make, all were bent upon to see others succeed and with the result, contacts of all came to rescue while launching the IPO of our champions. Because all started supporting each other by underwriting the same themselves and through their friends with the result the euphoria built was enough to have a domino effect and thus succeeded beyond belief.

During 2028-2030 out of 10 who had started the journey four were successful in launching their IPO's and all opened with premiums ranging from 20% to even 100% thus enriching the shareholders and management equally. All who were involved were too happy as all had a role to play in one way or the other in bringing out the same.

The journey was quite challenging but with the cooperation of financial institutions, who took pains to launch the same after being satisfied as to its feasibility and immense scope the company had, raised the morale of all.

Letters and emails with thank you notes were sent to all involved who made the same successful, and the management had understood that on their shoulder responsibility is even more now to keep the momentum going and they wowed among themselves to be more disciplined in future in taking care of all involved and show better results in the coming years.

With the IPO funds coming for the expansion, as per plan, now the projections were even more aggressive incorporating the AI and robotics technology to improve hygiene and quality – cost cutting besides aggressive marketing budget highlighting the same to grow a healthy bottom line.

All who succeeded were following the guidelines set by Mr Avinash Nispaksh, who being the MD of Champions Click N Connect himself had succeeded in bringing out the IPO of Champions Click N Connect Limited.

Instead of hitting the target of 3 lakh members as projected for the third year the progress was astonishing as on all fronts the work was initiated be it social media, shareholders of various companies – students of colleges and other institutions. The major chunk of members came from demat holders and thus the membership reached the level of 5 million members and is increasing even more every day by the time the IPO was launched.

The IPO's success brought the company to a greater limelight thus the domino effect taking place to increase the bottom line miraculously to the surprise of shareholders, management and the workforce alike.

The valuation of the company being in its infancy stage came down to staggering in many billions.

None of the champions could ever dream of reaching this stage but for the guidance and secret they understood from going through the book and following the principles mentioned there-in.

Conclusion

Making millions is not a challenging one from the share market as thousands or millions would be making and have made the same with patience either on long term or short term.

However, to understand that the vehicle called stock market is a lift for the aspiring entrepreneurs to make use of the same and become billionaires in the shortest of time.

Frankly speaking when I discussed the subject with my mentor, I wanted to make the heading how to make billions from the stock market? But he suggested the book will fail as no one would believe it, so I had to agree and started with how to make millions from the stock market, and his advice helped me to divide the book in two parts – which you have gone through.

Are you interested in being one to follow the same guidelines and succeed?

Knowledge is not wisdom but application of it is. Real wisdom lies in application of the same with hard and smart work. Disciplined approach with good habits, consistency and persistence is the key.

Mentor is important in the journey to succeed as his experience will help you cross or overcome the hurdles which are invisible to you.

Happy billionaire journey. Law of attraction – money is there waiting for you to be plucked from the universe.

Secret lies in the stock market and initiating the first step.

Wish you all the best and wait for your admission on auto mode in a billionaire club!

Wish you all the best and "Billionaire club management and its members" are waiting to welcome you!

The end!

No, it is the beginning of a new journey as a spiritual person –as a giver!

Money had lost its glitter while chasing dreams.

❑